W9-CXZ-867

THE MUST
OF MURDER

THE MUST
OF MURDER

•

Neta Seffer

AVALON BOOKS
NEW YORK

Published by Thomas Bouregy & Co., Inc.
160 Madison Avenue, New York, NY 10016

Library of Congress Cataloging-in-Publication Data

Seffer, Neta.
  The must of murder / Neta Seffer.
      p. cm.
  ISBN 978-0-8034-7758-2 (hardcover : acid-free paper)
  1. Women authors—Fiction.   2. Americans—Italy—
Fiction.   3. Murder—Investigation—Fiction.
4. Tuscany (Italy)—Fiction.   I. Title.
  PS3619.E365M87 2010
  813'.6—dc22   2009045213

PRINTED IN THE UNITED STATES OF AMERICA
ON ACID-FREE PAPER
BY HADDON CRAFTSMEN, BLOOMSBURG, PENNSYLVANIA

For Steve, Dov, Lev, and Gidon

Praise the bridge that carries you over.

I want to thank those who have been a bridge for me in my work and my life. In Italy, they have given me friendship, food, much laughter, and fine conversation. Welcoming me into their culture, they have shared their lives and homes, their knowledge, ideas, and perspectives, all the while patient as I fumbled along in a second language: The Zennaro family: Pino, Annalisa, Lorenzo, Rina; Gianni D'Este Widman; Umberto Sartori; the Nizzi family and grandparents: Roberto, Angela, Martina, Elisa, Bruno, Filomena; Elena Servi; Luigi Cerroni; the Cini family: Concetta, Francesco, Stefania, Massimo; Carlo Fe; Annamaria Liberati; Cinthia Astori; Franco Paioletti; Sue Reese and Oliver Howlett; and Antoinetta Cini.

In the United States, I owe a large debt to the Utah Humanities Council for supporting my research in Italy through the Albert J. Colton Award, and to Lee Austin of KUSU-FM, Logan, Utah, and Doug Fabrizio, KUER-FM, Salt Lake City, both of whom enthusiastically encourages my commentaries, on Italy or otherwise. My friend and colleague, historian Anne M. Butler, has supported and guided me for many years. Her work has been a model of fine scholarship, personal grace, and elegance in the written word. I also want to thank my editor, Chelsea Gilmore, who, with good-spirited attention has ushered me over into this new genre of work.

Love and thanks to Coral, Harper, Jerry, Mary, Dana, and Joe who nurtured me, and last, I thank Steve, for the long walks and the many talks about this book and other writings, and my children: Dov, Lev, and Gidon, who have been the bridge into my best world of all.

Prologue

Leah Contarini bumped down the steps to the basement, ignored the dirty laundry on the floor next to the washing machine, and opened the door to her husband's office. When he looked up, she curled her index finger at him. "Mar-ga-reetas." She wiggled her eyebrows. "Sun's down. Canyon breeze is up. Chips and salsa are on the balcony."

Nick smiled. His wife was funny—and unpredictable. He shook his head.

"Can't do it. If I drink margaritas now, I'll be blotto for the rest of the evening."

"Not margaritas, just margarita. Come on." She whined like a six year old, twisting her shoulders and rolling her eyes.

Nick laughed. "Ever the writer! I could have sworn you said margaritas."

She had, but pretended not to, and rushed on. "Just one, come on. And then I'll be good and fix dinner while you work."

She did a little dance of goodwilled impatience. "Then we'll eat, read, and then later, you can tell me all about your sabbatical proposal and I will tell you about the article I'm going to write on Scansansiano while we're there."

He held out his arms to her. She moved into them, and he buried his face in her stomach. "I like the plan."

"Good!"

"But"—he dropped his arms and they both turned to stare at the computer screen—"I'm tired of this proposal. You'd think I'd proved myself enough already without having to go through it all again. It takes so much damn time."

She kissed him on the head, her arm draped around his shoulder. "Mornings are wiser than evenings. Work 'til dinner, then let it go until tomorrow. I'm done with the article for *Traveling!*, so in the morning I can go over what you've already written while you continue with the last part, and when I'm finished, we'll trade: You can read over my piece and I'll read over the last part of yours. Okay?"

"Okay."

She kissed him again on the top of the head.

* * *

Later they lay in bed talking. Leah leaned up on her elbow. "Okay. I got you to have the margarita, so now let's talk about the Befania." She settled her head on his chest.

"You really want to hear this stuff?"

"Of course I want to hear it."

"What a perfect little academic wife you are!"

She poked him in the side. "Yes. And a perfect little travel writer too, with a perfect little contract for another piece about Scansansiano that will help pay for the perfect little sabbatical." She poked him again. "Lecture please!"

He adjusted the pillow. "Not so much lecture as questions."

"Just like the storyteller says: It's the questions that bring us together and the answers that separate us."

She liked Nick's Socratic method of teaching—the way his students interacted with each other and worked their brains instead of hovering, heads bent, frantically scribbling down every word he said, while what he was actually saying dissipated in the stuffy air of the classroom.

Nick fell silent for a minute while he thought about what to say. Leah waited, watching the curtains billowing in the breeze that flowed through the open windows.

"Okay," Nick's face had the faraway look common to him when he discussed his work. "These are the questions: What does this form of Epiphany mean to the community? Why does it take place in southern Tuscany and not in other parts of Italy? Did today's Befania evolve from some Pagan festival?"

"Must have." She shifted her head to look up at him in the dim light of street light that edged through the curtains.

He dropped his arm close around her. "Yes, but I ask because it leads to what festival? And why an old woman as the main character, the Befana? And why not an actual woman, rather than a man dressed as a woman? And when did she acquire a husband? And a daughter? And what about the cities, where the Befana really is just a gift giver, instead of like Scansansiano, where she comes to make music and dance and then take away food? And why is it agricultural? And how is the festival evolving? Does the revival of the Befania in the theater mean an end of the actual one in the countryside? What does the Befania do for the communities that practice it? What will they lose if it fades away? What do the different practices say about the concept of regions in Italy?"

Pressed against Nick, flesh to flesh, Leah could feel the excitement in the muscles of his chest and arm, and she snuggled even closer, happy to hear him talk about his work.

"Leah, sorry, but I've got to get up and write some things in my notebook."

"Okay. See you in the morning." She yawned, rolled over, and was asleep before he had turned on the light in the spare bedroom.

In her dream, Leah was already in Scansansiano, sitting at the Antoninis' table, where, on earlier research and writing trips, she had enjoyed countless Sunday dinners and hours of conversation. Then, suddenly, from their friends' table, she was alone, walking one of the vie cave, the steep-sided Etruscan trails carved deep into the tufa stone, canopied by thick forests. Excited, apprehensive, she moved upward, quickening her pace as she passed the wide maws of the burial caves along the rough way. Something—or someone—was after her.

The following morning, Leah lingered on the balcony over coffee. The dream had intensified the fear she always felt on the vie cave. She shook her head to dispel the sensation and stood, whisking her cup from the little wooden table in front of her. "I'm nuts!" she said to the red-shafted flicker spearing the grass for food.

Chapter One

An early January chill seeped under Leah's jacket, encircled her narrow waist, and ran down her arms. Above the via cava it was sunny, but in the dim light of the path she shivered from the cold and from the exciting tinge of fear that always accompanied her when she was here alone.

She breathed deeply, filling her lungs with the crisp wet air, and picked up her pace. The chill, and the exertion of the upward ascent, reminded her of her first long runs up Fall Creek through the thick Oregon forests. Today, the dense vegetation and overhanging trees of the Etruscan trail were much the same, and she felt an immense pleasure at her memories of hiking and running in the Oregon wilderness.

A few photos would complete the article she was writing about the vie cave, and would give her plenty of time to e-mail the piece to *On The Go And Free!* magazine before the deadline, which was still a few days away. Finished with the article, she could concentrate on helping Nick with his food and culture research on the Befania that would be taking place that night.

She had left the house angry. Camera savvy and having promised to take the photos for her piece, Nick had reneged that morning on his promise to go with her. Then, just after, their daughter Sara had phoned to say that she and her fiancé, Jonathan, were postponing the wedding. Leah envisioned the dozens of long-distance phone calls it would take to help her daughter cancel caterers, hotel rooms, and the expansive private garden perched above the Oregon coast.

Now, breathing rhythmically and hard as she made her way upward, she struggled to control her emotions. Objectively, she realized she could handle all of it on her own, and she knew that with some time to herself, she would calm down. She was like that: her anger would flare and then, given a few hours or a day or two, her resentment would abate and that would be the end of it. But just now, having bounded down the steep stone steps from the apartment and reaching the trail, she was still vexed with Nick, glad to be away from him and the phone, and was looking forward to experimenting with the new camera.

A rock shifted above her. Startled, she stopped and looked up, feeling her neck muscles tensing. The rock walls that bounded the trail loomed fifty feet over her small frame, and were so close on either side that by stretching her arms she could touch both of the sheer flanks at once.

Staring up at the holm oak and vine dangling from the earth edges at the top of the walls, Leah listened. A slight breeze meandered through the spiked ferns that sprung like fingers from the cracks in the rocks. She watched the leaves of the trees sway above her.

Maybe a squirrel. She expelled a sudden breath and smiled at her own fear, shaking her head. A few dark curls slipped from beneath her navy wool hat, and she reached to brush them away before she started upward once again humming "Seven Golden Daffodils," a song a friend used to sing. The morning mist cooled her face, and she was happy.

At the line in the song "I can show you morning on a thousand hills," she broke into full voice, opening her arms as if to gather in to herself the forest and tree-lined gorge that led seaward through the land below her. A thousand hills: Tuscany.

The stubby oak and red-berried bushes created a gloomy light over the trail, which was punctuated every few yards by the gaping mouths of burial caves; broad, low–ceilinged grottos with narrow biers carved into the stone walls. These damp sanctums had been plundered to a musty emptiness centuries ago by foreign visitors and locals alike. Still, they seemed to Leah to be inhabited, and she shivered at the memory of entering them, even when Nick was with her.

Every few yards another dark maw opened on her right or her left and with each breath she sucked in the dank, fetid odor. She imagined the smells to be the remnant scent of dead Etruscans hovering invisibly in, over, and around the caves where they had once lain on the stone slabs. She felt not fear, but the unearthly presence of history of both the distant and recent past, of the stories that lay below the viewed reality, as if those stories might come alive unexpectedly in front of her. It was the uncanny sense that other lives were being lived just at the edge of her peripheral vision.

She had been in the wine cellars, the famous cantinas, in town, but they elicited a gentler sense of the emptiness of these caves. The cantinas pocked the sheer walls under the houses of Scansansiano and were dark as well, and hewn from the same stone, though they had not been used for burial. Those on the northern edge of town retained an exact, cool 11 degrees Centigrade year round, a perfect and consistent temperature for wine-making and preservation; places where, walking along the road, you could be invited in to share a glass of the past year's vintage. She had heard sons and daughters of the older people in town hoping someday to be willed one of those caves, so that they in turn could brag about the delicate local wine from their own cantinas, and of an evening offer friends a glass of the pure and powerful *fragolino*.

The thought of the cantinas elicited an image of the Etruscans, surrounded by relatives, eating and drinking the wine that over the centuries had evolved into the famous Brunello di Montalcino or the smooth Morellino di Scansano. Those ancient peoples in their flowing robes, drinking wine and laughing *were* still present all around, Leah was certain, and they were staring out at her now from the enormous black caverns along the sides of the trail. She could sense the workers who had patiently chipped the pathways and the caverns out of this warren of volcanic tufa gorges. The enclosed palisades and the curved walls of the caves still showed the embedded, sweeping pattern of the double-edged tool the laborers had used to make them.

With a nervous gesture, Leah pulled off her hat, tossed her long black curls out of her face, and then tucked her hair once again under her stocking cap.

At the lip of each depression in the trail, Leah placed her feet carefully, thinking of the thousands of donkeys' hooves that had worn these steps in the smooth stone. For centuries, the little beasts had been carrying wood and produce up and down, to and from the fields on the flat lands above the gorge of the Bieta River where she walked.

In spots where the sun could not reach, the walls of

the pathways were covered with a thick, brilliant green moss, soft and moist to the touch. Along the undercuts at the bottom of the walls, water seeped through dirt-filled cracks and dripped into the narrow slit of a side channel that directed rain and run-off through openings in the walls toward the scattered bits of flat, treeless spaces that dotted the thick forests.

The rivulets of rain water tumbled gently from hollow to hollow and wet Leah's shoes. Taking a quick step up a broken spot in the trail, she slipped on moss and threw her hand out against the rock wall just in time to prevent herself from falling. She had neglected to wear gloves, and her hands were red, stiff from the cold and sensitive to the scabrous rock.

As she righted herself, the camera swung into a clump of cyclamen, and she jerked back to prevent it from getting wet. She noticed one of the buds of the pure white flower was about to bloom, unusually early, and decided to take a photo of it. It would be a good chance to try the macrosetting.

Holding steady, Leah pressed the shutter release. When she brought the camera up to look at the picture, it showed not the flower, but the ground just in front of her feet, and she realized there had been a delay between the moment she pressed the release and the moment the picture had been taken.

She shook her head and snorted. For an instant she considered trying the shot again, but then decided to go on and deal with the macrosetting another time.

Within minutes she reached one of the high points in the trail, where, to her right, just at a break in the wall, she stepped out on a broad overhang of rock that centuries before had been chiseled and chipped away to form a flat floor with seats—thrones actually—around the edges, with armrests and all.

Across the gorge on the other side of the Bieta River, which twisted off toward its source in the northeast, she regarded a field of intense green winter wheat joined by another of the vie cave to a meadow at the crest of the high tableland, where a flock of sheep was grazing in the winter sun. After the previous night's downpour, the sky was pure cerulean, with frothy white clouds wafting toward the northeast.

Below her the steep slopes were covered with a thick forest, an entangled mass of brush, bamboo breaks, and slender trees jutting skyward. She edged toward the unfenced lip of the rock, remembering her father's fear of heights, even though he was a master carpenter and often worked on the roofs of the houses he was building.

Craning her neck, but careful to keep away from the edge, Leah peered downward at the forest of oak and underbrush covering the steep descent to the river. The foliage glistened from the previous night's rain. Straightening, she carefully stepped back. She snapped several photos and turned to gaze in all directions. Below her, she spied another flat outcrop along a narrow trail that twisted off to the right from the one by which she had come, and she realized that from the lower outcrop she could get a good shot of the whole of the table rock on which she was standing. It would perfectly demonstrate the sheer drop and the thick forests of what had been one of the centers of Etruscan civilization, and would make clear for the readers how hidden the vie cave actually were to the casual eye. She imagined a photo of the wooded side of the gorge, with an overlay red line to trace at least one of the vie.

Cheered by the prospect of a perfect shot, Leah followed the thread of trail downward, squeezed through a hole between two bushes, and stepped out onto the rock she had seen from above. With this photo, and one of the underground necropoles she and Nick had reasoned would make a good shot, she knew the editor would be excited.

She checked the "scene" setting, held steady, and, allowing for the short lapse between the time she clicked the shutter and the time the photo registered, she focused on the table rock above and snapped, holding the camera firmly in place once it clicked.

In the two or three seconds it took the camera to click and flash, Leah saw two figures arguing on the table rock. The shorter of the two, wearing dark clothing and a broad-brimmed hat, was pushing the other in the chest. The second, dressed like a laborer in blue coveralls, stumbled backward toward the edge of the rock, and the first gave one last, powerful push.

The man in coveralls catapulted into the air, a thrown

doll. His arms and legs flayed for purchase, but found none, and his scream was lost in the vast expanse of emptiness as he fell toward the steep forest floor.

At the same moment she saw the man topple over the edge, Leah saw the other one turn, scanning the brush and outcrops, and she realized that he had caught a glimpse of her flash. She watched in disbelief as he whirled around, and knew he was coming for her.

Chapter Two

In the apartment, Nick stared out the window at Rondini Falls far below him on the Bieta River. If he opened the window, he knew he would hear the pleasant, distant rumble of the falls, but he did not want to hear it—or anything. He wanted to sleep. Lying on his stomach on the bed, he tucked his face into his arm, closed his eyes and squinted, trying to shut out the mind whirl. Tonight was supposed to be the culmination of eleven months' preparation for his last research before the book.

"One lousy nap, for God's sake!" He spit the words through his teeth, then flipped onto his back and pulled the duvet over himself. There was a loud crack as a metal leg of the bed broke.

"Damn it! Lousy bed!"

He rolled out, stood, and kicked at the other, good leg of the offending furniture, emitting a high-pitched yell when his bare foot met the metal.

He had lain on the bed and risen five times since Leah left, but sleep would not come. He had checked his tape recorder a dozen times, had gone over his camera an equal number, had made a list of questions he could ask the participants and mulled over every bit of information about the Befania that he could remember.

Wandering into the bathroom, he leaned over the sink to look at himself in the mirror, having carefully closed the door behind him, as if there were someone to see this slight vanity. He ran his fingers vigorously through his wavy, dark blond hair to clear his mind, and then tilted his head to inspect his chin, deciding he should shave before he left in the evening to tour the local farmhouses with the members and musicians of the Befania troupe. He looked forward to driving from one farmhouse to the next, stopping to sing, dance, eat, and drink at each one, but for now he couldn't concentrate, and as he regarded himself in the mirror, his frustration seemed to intensify the green in his eyes and the creases in his forehead.

Deciding to take another look at the notes from the last year's Befania and the new notes he had entered in the computer, he turned back into the living room and sat at his desk. Glancing down, he could see that the pile of books he had arranged as a makeshift set-up to hold the heavy transformer in the outlet was twisted.

When he bent to straighten the books, he bumped the table, pushing the leg against the transformer, which flipped out of the wall, prongs bent to the side from the force of the table leg.

"Damn it!"

Nick picked up the transformer and pressed and pulled at the prongs to straighten them, but just as they appeared to be righted, one of the prongs pulled loose. "Damn it! Damn it! Damn it!" He threw the transformer to the floor, remembering and swiveling just in time to catch the computer before it tipped off the table.

"Okay. Okay. Deep breaths."

After carefully setting the computer securely on the table, he stood and walked in circles around the room, breathing heavily in and out. The problem wasn't the research on the festival. It wasn't his research on festivals in general, nor was it his equipment that was frustrating him. It wasn't even the pressure of finishing the research, writing the book, and finally ending the arduous process of attaining full professor—it was Leah.

Or it was the circumstance of both of them having deadlines at the same time. He pushed the thought out of his mind, resisting the obvious. He *felt* it was Leah's fault he couldn't sleep, and he had directed his anger at her for asking him to come through on his promise when his own preparation had taken more time than he thought it would.

A friend who had been a Peace Corps volunteer with

Leah in West Africa, well before Nick knew her, had told Nick that one day during their stint they had decided to go horseback riding in the Sahara. He said that Leah had borrowed a little Arabian stallion, a two-year-old, and she was unable to handle it. Each time she mounted the horse, it bucked her off, and each time she rose to her knees and then her feet, dusted the sand off her clothes, grabbed the mane, and remounted. And the horse bucked her off again. The friend told him that she tried all morning, into the heat of midday until, by early afternoon, both she and the horse were too exhausted to continue.

Nick sat in a chair at the table next to the bed and rubbed his foot. Remembering his friend's story about Leah and the horse, he mulled over the quality of Leah's stubbornness. He loved her for it, even when it irritated him, and he now felt ashamed of himself for the way he had taunted her, with pettiness of spirit, just before she walked out the door. His last words, unreasonable and spiteful, were that she should go out and play tourist. The words had flown out of his mouth; as soon as he said them he wished he could retrieve them from the wind, but Leah had tossed her head and bounded down the wide stone stairway leading from their apartment toward the gorge, and he was too late. He had stood at the doorway and watched the tip of her hat disappear as she rounded the curve. Frustrated with himself, and with her, he had stepped back into the house, slamming the door behind him.

The little apartment they had rented just below Piazza Portarini was usually a refuge for him. Their two little rooms hung over the gorge just above the fork where the Bieta and Lavini Rivers met, and with a glance out the window, Nick could see for miles toward San Giorgio and Bareno, other originally Etruscan villages. But today, the house was no retreat.

He sat at his desk in front of the computer staring at his notes. The walls of the apartment retained moisture, and the winter cold had created a perpetual chill that hung like a damp blanket in the rooms. He leaned over and punched the pellet stove up a notch. It would take a minute to kick in, and he shivered as he tried to concentrate on what he expected to see at the coming night's events.

Within a few minutes, compelled to motion by his frustration, he rose, put the kettle on for tea, and waited until it fumed at the spout. With a sharp knife he sliced a lemon, squeezed the tart juice into the cup as the tea steeped, added a full tablespoon of the local thick brown honey, and carried the cup to the table.

Leah. Publishing this book on the Befania would carry him on to full professor. Once done, he could relax and continue the research he loved without worry about moving up another notch at the university.

But Leah. Nick thought of her soft brown eyes, and of her alone on the vie cave trying for the best pictures and was suddenly overcome by his own foolishness, wishing he hadn't suggested the necropolis, where he was sure she would go even if they were eerie. Leaving the cup steaming on the wooden table, he grabbed his jacket off the hook by the door and headed down the mottled stone steps after her.

Chapter Three

The camera banged against Leah's leg as she bounded pell-mell down the rock trail. With every step she felt her foot slip and grasp. Instinctively, she stiffened her legs and sucked air; it was as if she were in one of the dreams of impotence that had disturbed her childhood sleep: A wild boar was chasing her, and all she had to do was lift her leg and step over the fence in front of her, but weighted by fear, her legs were heavy as stone, and she moved in excruciatingly slow motion with the breath of the boar at her neck.

Now, trembling, skidding along the wet trail, she smacked her palms against the rock wall to steady herself as she passed. Except for the clink of a loose rock behind her, she could not hear the killer, but she knew he was close, and she had seen what he could do.

21

Ahead, the rock wall opened onto a small grassy field perched above the gorge. A sign at the edge of the opening signaled in Italian and English, NECROPOLIS, ETRUSCAN BURIAL GROUNDS. It was the place Nick had suggested she photograph. With the lucidity of terror, she spotted impressions in the fresh earth at the bottom of the sign and recognized the snout marks of cinghiale, the tusked boars that lived in these thick woods, rooting and feeding off the acorns of the holm oak.

She gasped thinking there was a drift of boars nearby, but there was no choice. Lurching headlong through the opening, she broke into the field only a few steps from two picnic tables that were set on a patch of grass. To the side of them, a wooden fence surrounded three deep dromos, the sunken passages that led into the burial caves. She hesitated at the first, but saw it was filled with murky water that reached three feet up the wall of the entryway. The twisted arms of a wild raspberry bush covered the opening of the second.

The third was dry. She grabbed the top wooden railing, ducked under, and dropped into the narrow opening.

For an instant, staring into the black mouth of the cave, she faltered. Then, hearing another rock tumble on the pathway, she plunged into the darkness.

Light. Light. Her mind was frenzied. *The camera flash.* She pressed the shutter release and stamped the ground in terrified impatience in the seconds before the flash went off, but in the moment it did, she caught a glimpse of a low ledge with a wide deep hole beneath it. The light gone now, she dropped to her knees and scrambled toward the opening, banging her shoulder against the ledge before she fell flat and edged into the tight space, darker even than the dark of the cave.

The must of death was strong, and she gagged. Grabbing her hat off her head, she held it tightly over her mouth to muffle the sound, breathing deeply through her nose. The hat stifled her breath and she swallowed her gorge to keep from vomiting outright, pushing herself farther into the space until she bumped against the back of the little alcove that she hoped would save her.

Pulling in the air through the loose weave of her hat, Leah forced herself to take long, slow breaths. The cave was silent.

Then, footsteps.

And panting.

The run had winded him. His breathing was heavy like that of a dog, he gasped in an agonizing rhythm that echoed in her ears. In a macabre counterpoint to his breath, he prodded the floor and crevices of the cave with a long stick. The thin, brittle wood rasped against the tufa, jittered along the pocked walls, and, through her hat, with each breath, Leah smelled the dust the killer raised as he swept the stick back and forth.

The cave walls amplified the sound of his breathing. Leah squeezed her eyes shut trying to dampen the deafening sound. She crammed her hat hard over her mouth, stifling the thunder of her own breathing, tilted her chin downward, attempting to stop the light-headed sensation she felt from lack of oxygen. Her chest rose and fell and her stomach muscles worked against her legs, which she had drawn tight to her chest.

As he came closer, she was tempted to crawl out, to get it over with. Her heart was pounding and fear curled through her limbs, raising the bile in her throat once again. He was going to kill her, and she struggled against a terrible impatience for the final blow. The relief of being out of his reach, of stopping the horrible rhythm of his breathing, even if it meant going over the cliff, enticed her almost beyond resistance.

Nick. Sara. She ached to ask forgiveness of Nick, to see Sara one last time.

The faint, high pitch of a whistle curled into the opening of the cave. Sucking air, Leah realized it was Nick, blowing on the silver whistle she had bought and given him in Portugal on a vacation they had taken to Cascais. Later, he had given her one as well, one that he bought on a trip with his friend Adam in Spain. Both she and Nick wore the whistles when they went hiking; hers hung round her neck now, and she lowered her hand carefully to her chest, tempted to pull the little engraved instrument to her mouth, to be saved, but aware that the killer would probably get to her first, guided directly to her by the sound.

The air of the cave, the darkness, trembled with a thick, hesistant silence; the killer had to have heard the whistle as well. She imagined him leaning toward the sound, straining to decipher whether or not he was in danger of being discovered.

She heard Nick blow again, the high pitch closer than before.

Leah shivered and grasped the delicate weight of the whistle, sliding it slowly up her chest, as if for comfort, though she knew she could not use it. She held it close in the little depression at the base of her neck, pursing her lips to release each breath with the slightest vibration possible, willing each one unheard.

She waited.

Suddenly, the killer emitted a loud grunt, and Leah heard him rush away, his hurried footsteps then fading as he left the cave and climbed back to the earth above.

Silence.

She waited for another call from Nick's whistle. She counted the seconds. A minute. Two. Three. Nothing.

A trick. In her fear she struggled to think straight, clutching her own whistle in her fist. *Wait. Just wait.*

Stomach churning, she felt her gorge rise once again, and this time she could not stop herself. She tilted her head to the side and vomited in the dust, prodding the half-digested food away from her face with the back of her hand. Stifling her sobs, she inhaled and exhaled as deeply as she could, compelling herself to be calm as she strained to hear some sign that the killer was still there.

Nothing.

Panting into her hat, she waited.

The whistle sounded nearby. Footsteps again. She pressed her hat harder over her mouth.

Chapter Four

"Leah? You told me you'd be here, so don't hide, okay? Don't be angry."

Leah burst into loud sobs; gulping air, she clawed her way through the dirt, out of her hiding place and lurched toward Nick, whose form was just visible in the dim light of the cave opening. He staggered backward under her weight.

"Hey, what's going on?"

Her mouth moved like a dying salmon, and no words would come. She clung to him, trembling. Nick held her head to his chest and stroked her hair and back.

"It's okay. I'm here."

"Nick we're not safe. He could come back. He knows I'm here . . ."

"Who?"

"A man pushed another man off the table rock. I saw him. I took a picture of it. I saw him. I didn't mean to. He shoved him off the table rock and the guy grabbed at the air and screamed, and it was just when I pressed the shutter release and I think I have a picture of it because there's a lapse, and now he's going to look for me and find me and kill me. He was here. He knew I was here."

"Slow down Leah."

He held her at arms' length, squeezing her arms tightly, fearful for her and feeling an edge of fear himself.

"Look at me, Leah."

He pulled her away from the opening of the cave into full sunlight and stared directly into her face, forcing her to concentrate on his eyes.

"Slow, baby, slow. You saw some guy push another guy off a cliff?"

"It's what I told you!" She jerked out of his grasp and shoved the camera toward him. "Look!"

Nick turned on the camera and pressed the review button. They hovered together over the tiny screen. A photo of the floor of the cave appeared on the screen.

"No, not that one! That's the one I took to get some light. Click it back one."

Nick pressed the return and a picture of the murder flashed onto the monitor. Clearly one man was shoving the other.

"Oh my God! The one in the coveralls looks like Giulio."

"Let me see." She reached for the photo. "Oh no! I didn't recognize him."

"I'm certain. He's the guy who runs the knickknack shop with Silvio, just off the piazza, right? And he always wears coveralls. The other one's too dark to tell."

Nick pulled Leah close to him again. "Do you think the killer recognized you?"

"I don't think so. If he had, I think he would have said my name in the cave, and I had all my hair tucked up in my hat and I'm wearing that coat I bought here, so I could've seemed Italian."

"Good. Okay, let's think. At least we can identify Giulio. Did you notice anything about the other one?

"Yeah . . ." She held him, thinking. "There was something glistening on his head, but he was too far away for me to tell what it was or for me to see his face, and then the flash caught his attention and that was when he came after me."

Nick squeezed her as tight as he dared; then, taking her arm, guided her up the slanting passageway toward the trail. "Let's go back. We'll stop at the police station, and you can tell Lieutenant Cavour the whole story."

Finding the police station locked, they walked arm in arm through the piazza, avoiding conversation with a quick wave at acquaintances, and hurried on to the apartment. Once inside standing in the middle of the kitchen, Nick encircled Leah in both arms and looked down, into her eyes.

"I'm sorry Lieutenant Cavour and his sergeant weren't there. But we can't do anything until they get back, so I think you should take a hot shower."

Leah opened her mouth to protest, but he put his finger to her lips, shaking his head. "No. A shower. We've got to slow down and figure out what to do."

She pulled back. "What do you mean 'What to do?' "

He ignored her question and paced back and forth, mumbling, thinking aloud and paying no attention to what she was saying.

"If Sergeant Gianicollo is out and Cavour is in the gorge and is going to be gone until tomorrow like the sign said, and the only emergency numbers are theirs, then there's nothing we can do until tomorrow; the secretary's off today, and I wouldn't tell her anyway." Nick looked at Leah and smiled. "You know her; she's that redheaded Scottish woman that's always in the bar gossiping."

He brushed his hand through the air over his head to indicate the secretary's hair.

"Thank God you had on that hat and the coat—and that you can run like Wilma Rudolph. Still, whoever this guy is, he's going to assume that you'll be telling everybody and that he'll soon find out who you are."

He reached for her, hugging her to him before he turned to pacing again. "Thank God you had on the hat and the jacket."

"You're repeating yourself, and I'm not one hundred percent certain that he didn't recognize me anyway."

Tears came to Nick's eyes. "I know it. I know it." He drew her to him again in a fierce hug, as if to protect her from the terror already past, and what could be the horror of the future.

"Listen, Leah. We can hope he won't be able to distinguish your clothes from anyone else's in town. It's reasonable, if not certain. And, I didn't pass him on the way coming up, so I'm figuring he continued up trail instead of coming down, like we did. I must have scared him off."

"How did you know I'd be there?"

"I didn't for sure, but remember, we were talking about seeing those caves last time, and you sounded so interested I figured you'd go there—anyway, that means that all he knows is that someone was up there with a bright blue jacket and a dark blue hat—and we'll put those in a sack in the dumpster so there's no chance he'll associate them with you. But for sure he'll be watching, and unless we're careful, he won't have any trouble figuring out what people are doing at the police station. The important thing is not to give him *any* clues."

"But the police won't know it's murder. They'll probably think the guy just fell."

"Look, whatever they think, they've found him—you heard Signora Luciapietra in the piazza—and for sure, they'll start an investigation. We'll go in tomorrow, relaxed, casual, and tell Miss Redhair we need to talk to the lieutenant about our visa. That's what she'll tell everyone—and when we get into Cavour's office, we close the door, tell him, and give him the disk from the camera. Then we can look at the photo close up."

"We could look at it now, on the computer."

"No, we can't." He blushed. "I screwed up the transformer. I didn't want to tell you just yet."

"But—"

"I'll get it fixed. There's a lot more to worry about than the article, so let it go, okay?"

"We could take it to Andrea. I saw him arguing with Signora Vianello in the piazza, just at the door to the camera shop. She was talking to the woman who owns the grocery store, and I heard her say she had been waiting and he was late!"

"Sounds like the signora. But you're rambling, stop and think: We can't take it to Andrea. He would print it and before long the news would be all over town. We can't show it to anyone but Cavour." Nick wrinkled his forehead. "For now, let's just go on as if things were normal. The lieutenant's a smart guy, discreet."

Nick fell silent, staring at the floor. "Listen, Francesca will be here before long. You'll be safe with the Antoninis tonight, and I'll see you there when our group comes round to their house."

Leah watched him. As angry as she got with his perpetual analyzing, his patient, thorough reasoning was one of the things she loved most in him.

Standing safely in front of Nick, it amazed her how fast thought could travel. In an instant of memory she experienced the excitement of finding the spot for a great photo, the initial disbelief at what she was seeing, the terror of the escape down the trail into the cave, and then the safe haven of Nick's arms. These events and the strangeness of love flitted across her mind: One man coldly evil, and another gentle. Her emotions spiraled through her heart, erupting in fear, gratitude, anger, and terror. Had she been identified? Was it a foolish hope? The fear morphed to anger, or perhaps they were the same thing. And perhaps she was still angry with Nick because he hadn't gone with her in the first place. Yet here she was, loving him. It was the way love worked: It would arise, burst, and then fade, leaving in its wake sometimes a sudden hot flow of passion or a soft cool moment of tenderness. All this in the tangled threads, all this wreathed with laughter.

She turned toward the bathroom, swiveled around, and looked back at Nick.

He raised his index finger to cut her off. "Don't. I know you want to jump in and go after the guy, and I know it seems heartless and I know it seems as if I want us to drop it now just so I don't miss the Befania."

Smiling, Leah watched him. He went on, as if to himself, without looking at her, marking each point by tapping his finger against the air. "And you're right, I suppose, but not totally. The guy is obviously hunting you and this plan is best. We're not leaving a corpse alone in the woods. We don't have access to the police now anyway, right? And you did understand what they were saying in the piazza as we came up, right? That

Leonardo was out hunting, they said, "alla caccia"—and found the guy himself? And he'll tell you all about it tonight when you're out there. And listen, we need to talk to the police before we say anything."

Leah interrupted his monologue. "But the Antoninis are our closest friends. And Leonardo did find him . . ."

Nick turned his attention to her and clasped her shoulders. "Leah, please don't be headstrong about this. They'll be upset, and if any word gets out about what you saw, it could endanger them too. It's the safest way. Remember that disaster training you took: The greatest good for the greatest number of people?"

"Oh, come on!"

He blushed. "Okay, that was a bit much. And it's true, this way I don't have to miss the Befania."

She hugged him. "I'll decide what to say when I get to the Antoninis. Now, would you mind bringing me a towel from downstairs?"

Nick grimaced. She would do what she wanted to do.

Chapter Five

A ndrea the photographer was running across the piazza. He could see Signora Vianello standing at the door
of his shop, impatiently shuffling from one foot to the
other. Her fur coat, which she wore in and out of season
to show off her wealth, was crouched on her broad,
heavy shoulders, and Andrea felt the sense of revulsion
at what he thought to be the persistent demonstration of
her wealth. A landowner, and him a shopkeeper.

Secondo, the so-called town idiot, stood nearby, grinning at the sight of Andrea's long legs, churning through
the air. Secondo's manner was to watch and speak little;
he liked seeing what people would do, particularly when
they were angry or upset. When, the evening before, the
two men in the bar had begun to argue, he was over-
joyed, grinning and dancing around the edge of the

35

crowd that had gathered, clapping his hands each time one would slam the other in the face with his fist. Secondo screeched in delight at times like this, and mostly, the townspeople ignored him.

Considering the haughty signora, Andrea thought, *Before long, you'll think differently about me, you old bag.*

His coat flying up behind him, he bounded toward her. "Coming, signora. Coming."

She watched him approach. He was a tall man, lanky, and ill-kempt, but not unattractive. He had never married, and though the signora liked him and had supported his work by buying his photos, she was at the same time wary of him, a little afraid. It was the way she sometimes glimpsed him looking at her, as if he were angry with her for some slight. It made no sense; she found his work beautiful, exquisite even, and almost every room in her house had at least one of his photos on the wall. But when he came close, she felt an uneasy tremor, as if he might hurt her physically. She chose to counteract her own unease with assertive behavior.

He arrived out of breath, panting. "I'm . . . sor-ry. I hope you'll forgive me. I . . . was de-layed."

She cringed. He had addressed her with the familiar form rather than the formal, and this infraction of good manners aggravated her anger. "Where have you been? And what's the matter? You're heaving, as if you've seen a ghost . . ." She looked him up and down. "Your tie is askew, and your feet are muddy."

Infuriated, Andrea controlled himself. She had no right to be nosey about his business, but he could not afford to demonstrate his anger. Flustered by his own emotions, he responded. "I . . . I . . . I was in a meeting."

"In the woods it appears!" She knew he was lying, and he knew she knew it, so she let it go. "I've been waiting twenty minutes!"

He regarded her without speaking. She wore a thick coating of face powder, dark clumped mascara, and garish red lipstick. Her cheeks were spotted with rouge in an attempt to make her cheek bones appear high, but below the rouge her skin sagged with the weight of years, making her a caricature rather than an actual woman.

She continued to whine, "I need the photos, now! Tonight. I promised my daughter to have them for their anniversary celebration. Catch your breath and let's get this done."

As she turned toward the door of the shop, he felt the urge to throttle her, but gritted his teeth, and was silent as he fumbled with the key. He fitted it in the door, shaking with anger, and turned the lock. "Wait here. I'll get the switch."

He moved carefully past a stand of tourist postcards that he had created for the summer visitors, and felt his way along the edge of his desk until he reached the coat stand against the wall, just beside the light switch. Illuminated, the bare bulb in the ceiling cast a dim light over the little room. Except for the desk and a small printer stand, the space was empty, but the walls

were covered with photos: historic shots of Scansansiano in the 1800s, two peasants sitting at the fountain
in the main piazza, a woman in her long, dark, cum-
bersome skirt hanging out laundry, a group of boys
frozen for posterity as they kicked a soccer ball back
and forth in the piazzetta. Intermingled with the historic photos were contemporary ones Andrea had
taken himself: A bird's eye view of the river below the
town, an artistic shot of a newly plowed field at the
edge of the forest. Stacks two to three feet deep of
framed photos and photos printed on aluminum leaned
against every wall.

"Why don't you clean this place? You have so many
beautiful pieces, Andrea. If it were real property, land,
you might care for it a little better, no?" Though she
meant to be tender, Andrea heard the condescending
tone that he hated.

"Real property? You don't think this is real property?
You think your land is any more valuable, that this is
just stuff?" He clenched his fists and glared at her. She
stepped back toward the door. Andrea moved after her,
snarling, "I'll soon have property worth twice as much
as yours."

"Don't address me in the familiar!" She was trembling, moving closer toward the door.

Andrea stopped, glancing nervously out the window.
"Never mind, signora, it's a joke." He smiled stiffly.
"I'll never have property like you. This, what you see
here, is all I have. It is as it is. But though it looks like a

mess to you I know each photo and I know where it is. As the English say, there's a method in my madness."

She stood with her hand on the doorknob, ready to escape, her voice barely a whisper. "Well, it still looks a chaos to me."

"Yes, but"—he took an envelope from his desk and handed it to her with an unctuous smile—"here are your photos—at my fingertips, no?"

She snatched the envelope from his hand. Her voice shook. "Yes, yes. Thank you. I'll pay you tomorrow. I . . . I'm late." She turned and rushed out the door, leaving it open behind her.

"Yes, tomorrow, you old hag." Andrea slumped in his chair; sweat dripped down his forehead. He wiped it away absentmindedly with his sleeve. "What a stupid, stupid woman. Oh, my God!"

Outside, Signora Vianello scurried toward her car. Just as she passed the bar facing the piazza, she noticed Angelina rush up the steps of the bar and flop down in a chair by the window with Giovanna, who was sitting at the corner table inside. Through the window she saw the two of them lean together in conversation, and the signora noted how scruffy they both looked. She shook her head. *How anybody ever buys real estate from that tough-looking woman is beyond me.* Of Giovanna she thought, *Such a mean and spiteful girl, who used to be so sweet before she got involved with those horrible men.* She hurried on.

The two young women were as much a part of the

piazza as the signora herself. Giovanna was the daughter of a man who, in his youth, had left, eager for a new life of wealth in America, and had returned disillusioned and angry. The anger persisted in his marriage to a woman who had been his elementary school classmate, and when the children came, one after the other, he began to take his frustrations out on them.

Angelina was from another town. The signora knew little about her, except that she was also in real estate and though the young woman appeared to think herself discreet, the signora—and everyone else in town who mattered—knew she was the mistress of another out-of-towner—"that buffoon" in Signora Vianello's mind—Italo. Angelina was an unattractive woman, who the signora thought must have been accustomed to spending hours outdoors. Her hair was perpetually scattered as if by the wind, even indoors, and her skin was tanned in a way the signora abhorred.

Why doesn't the girl at least wear a hat when she is out in order to protect her skin? None of them do these days. Sighing, she reached her car and opened the door.

Few people knew that Signora Vianello's inclination to wear her fur coat even on weekdays was not arrogance, but an atavistic response that had filtered down from her Venetian ancestors—ancestors accustomed to wealth and show. Many of the townspeople chided her behind her back for the coat her mother had passed down from her grandmother. The signora's age acted against her as well in the eyes of the younger townspeople. At seventy-six, she remembered the Scansansiano of earlier times when everyone dressed to go to the piazza, when the social hierarchy was clear, polite conversation was an art, and when a shopkeeper would not have spoken to her in the familiar, let alone in a rude manner.

She hurried on, her coat weighing her down, her generous heart obscured to others by the thick fur.

From inside the bar, Giovanna and Angelina saw her pass.

"Look at her," Giovanna quipped. "That fur coat! Will she ever get rid of the ratty thing?" She tapped nervously on the table and laughed.

"Forget about her. She's a nothing." Angelina frowned. "And anyway, look at you: silver crap all over your face. There isn't room for even one more earring, or nose ring or eyebrow ring or what the hell ever."

Giovanna ignored the remark about her piercings. "A nothing? Hardly, she's only the biggest landowner around."

"So who cares? Signora Seta's cantina is probably worth as much or more than Vianello's property."

"That much? Giulio—"

"Giulio . . . is a no-good lowlife."

"You're right. A jerk, a real jerk." Giovanna spat it out, looking down at the table and drumming again with her fingers. "Someday, he'll get what he deserves!"

Angelina grunted. "Think so?" She grinned. "What he deserves, huh? I didn't realize you hated him so much. I thought you two were an item."

"He uses people; he's no better than our fathers were." She turned aside, spitting on the floor.

"Hey!" the barmaid called out. "This isn't a barn! Get out of here if you're gonna act like that."

Giovanna turned to the barmaid. "Sorry! Sorry!" She rubbed her hands nervously along her thighs and gave a little wave. "I didn't really spit anything. It was just air."

"Well, don't even pretend. This is a decent place."

"Okay. Okay."

Angelina watched the exchange, then suddenly grasped Giovanna's arm. "Forget about Giulio. You don't need him. Italo will get the cantina, and then you'll come to work with us." She took the ashtray from the table and was holding it in both hands, rubbing it as if to polish it. "And you can go to Rome for what you need."

Giovanna stared at her, uncertain whether to be angry or laugh it off. Her laugh came out high and pinched. "So you know a few things. Okay. Allright." She pulled her arm away. "I'm calm."

The two women had known each other since confirmation classes with Don Alouso. Angelina had come to classes pale, thin, withdrawn, and nervous. Giovanna was attracted to her, later deciding that it was because she recognized in Angelina someone who had shared the experience of abuse. They had laughed and cried, even then, at the same things.

"Then we could have a real life here. Italo and I—and you working with us." Angelina dropped the ashtray with a loud bang.

Startled by the sudden crash, Giovanna burst out, "Right, right. Let's forget the old stuff, that's water under the bridge. Every house has its own passions, right?"

They sipped their coffee. Intensified by the glass of the window, the sun warmed them and they sat in a nervous silence, their hands moving continually, tapping the table, turning the ashtray.

It was Giovanna who broke the silence. "Listen, what's up with you? You look tired . . . and, sorry to say it, pretty ragged just now."

"I was out walking. And anyway, you don't look so good yourself. You tracked in mud when you came in. You just may get kicked out of here pretty soon."

Giovanna glanced down at her shoes. "Damn it!"

"Come on. I was joking. They're not that bad."

"I was . . . I was down on the steps below town; I dropped something yesterday."

"Yeah, right. You were doin' a deal, weren't you?"

"I wasn't!"

"Shtt! Okay, okay."

"How come you're not working? Nobody buying real estate?"

"Who cares? I gave myself the day off so I could rest."

"Well good for you!" Giovanna's voice was strained. She was struggling to stay in control, but her words, it seemed by their own volition, were tight, clipped and she spoke in the rough Italian she had learned at home, her thoughts scattered. "I wish I had a dog, but the only place to walk one would be the vie cave and I *never* go there, *never*!"

"Geez, okay. You never go there."

"Those trails are too blasted eerie." She was rambling. "I mean, even during the day, and anyway, living in the center of town I couldn't have a dog."

"So, let me sell you an apartment further out." Angelina threw both arms out, palms up, and grinned. "What's with the dog idea, anyway?"

Giovanna rolled her eyes with a slight tilt of her head, making her expansive hoop earrings wobble against her neck. She ignored Angelina's question. "Yeah, right. As if I had the money for an apartment. Anyway, how's Italo?"

Angelina smiled a slow, sinuous smile. "Change of subject? You're really distracted today. Okay. Italo's fine."

"From the look on your face, I'd say he is." Laughing, Giovanna poked Angelina's arm.

"Really, he is." She paused. "And don't look at me like that." Her face reddened in anger.

"Well, he reminds me of your father."

"Woooo! You're way off base. He's nothing like my ol' man. He's never hit me . . . and he never will."

"Famous last words!"

"Ah, shut up. You don't know anything about him. He's a lot of talk, but a real fluff at heart."

"Yeah? Well, I saw him kick a dog almost to death when it came at him one day on the piazza."

"Well a dog's different than a man, stupid."

"It's meanness all the same."

"You're an idiot. He does stuff like invite me to go to one of the autumn festivals"—she looked off as if in a dream—"they are the best . . ."

Giovanna leaned forward, enchanted by the surprisingly tender vision Angelina expressed.

". . . not just the harvest festival itself, but the fields in the fall, the vines heavy with the fruit . . ." She gazed out the window, as if she were searching for a sight of the fields. There were tears in her eyes.

"My God," Giovanna exclaimed, embarrassed by Angelina's show of emotion. "What are you crying about anyway? You said he's good to you."

"Yes, but . . ." Angelina grasped Giovanna by the arm, her eyes suddenly wild. "Giovanna, listen . . . did you ever do something you wish you hadn't done, but you couldn't take it back?"

"Stop it! You're hurting my arm." Giovanna pulled roughly away and charged into a tirade, furious with the pain. "And don't get started on that old stuff again. I can see it in your eyes, damn it. Your dad was who he was, and he did what *he* did. We've talked about this a hundred times. I want to forget what happened to me; I want to forget how I just want to kill someone, and I wish you'd forget what happened to you, so that we can just be friends and not be talking all the time about our hateful abusive fathers. Men! My God! It wasn't my fault and it wasn't yours; you were a kid and you couldn't have stopped him. You were a *kid*!" Giovanna shouted the word and the others in the bar turned to look. Her face turned red; she lowered her voice to a barely audible whisper. "Allright? So let it go. You've got Italo; he doesn't lie to you, and that's a hell of a lot more than a lot of us have."

Angelina sat up straight in her chair and wiped her eyes, staring at Giovanna as she brushed the tears away from her cheeks and chin. She cleared her throat. "You're right. What's done is done . . . and I can't change what happened. We're alike in that, and I didn't do it because I wanted to."

Angelina fell silent, looking at the floor as if she had dropped something. "I'm content to be his mistress. I actually like it that way. I don't want any sniveling little kids around, and I don't want a husband. I want just what I've got—a lover, to buy me a nice meal, take me on a vacation now and then. Somebody who has no say over my work."

"That's right. That's how we both have to deal with it. We—"

"I went to school with his wife, you know. She knows about me and Italo, but we go along; she stays down on the coast at their house and I stay here. I couldn't stand it though if he started up with some other woman." She had picked up the ashtray again and was turning it round and round in her hands, distracted. "Italo will get the cantina for the restaurant, and then we'll have a real life here."

"Don't be so sure about the cantina. There's Giulio you know, and then Andrea is next in line." She emitted a rude guffaw. "Unless Giulio is back in the doghouse— like I hope he is—and Andrea's in first place in Signora Seta's affections again. From the scuttlebutt it seems like the Signora wavers on it every day."

"It will work out." Angelina placed the ashtray directly in the center of the table and twirled it around.

"I guess things usually do."

"Andrea's the nicer. He'll be the one to inherit and all he wants are Signora Seta's old photos; he'll sell the cantina, Italo will buy it, and then Italo and I will have a life together."

"Dream on, sweetie. You said that, and you're right about Andrea being the nicer. But like I said, Giulio is a total miscreant, and Signora Seta is a wild card, so who knows which way she'll go?"

"Right. Who knows?" Angelina smiled.

Chapter Six

By late afternoon the news of Giulio's death had spread through town. There was a knock on the door at Nick's and Leah's, and Nick opened it to Francesca Antonini, the teenage daughter of their friends, Leonardo Antonini and Anna Pellini. Francesca's long dark hair twisted in the wind, and her face was creased with concern. She leaned forward as if to enter, but hesitated.

"Come, Francesca." She stared at him, and Nick smacked his forehead with his palm and switched to Italian. "Please come in." He motioned to the small flowered couch that faced the kitchen side of the room. "How's your dad?"

"Such a terrible thing," She said, stepping inside.

Nick glanced at Leah. "Signora Benvenuto stopped

by and she told us it was your dad that found him. What happened??"

"I don't know what could have happened." She shook her head slowly from side to side. "My dad was off work today, out hunting. He said he heard a scream and looked up to a see a man grasping at the air and then crash through the trees. He'll tell you about it when we get there." Tears pooled in her eyes.

"I'm sorry; I didn't mean to make you cry." Nick gave her a brief hug and kissed the top of her head.

She smiled at him weakly. "It's nothing. I'm vulnerable to your kindness right now. We've never had anything like this happen before, and my dad was saying that now they think maybe it was murder."

"Why do they think that?" Leah blurted.

Francesca jumped, surprised at Leah's sharp voice. "I don't know. Dad will tell you. He was the one who called Police Lieutenant Cavour, and he stayed with Giulio until they came."

"I'm sorry I startled you. It's all scombobulated."

The tears still glistening on her cheeks, Francesca burst into laughter at Leah's characteristic attempt to make an English word Italian. "Discombobulated," she corrected. "It's discombobulated."

Leah and Francesca walked through the dusk up the hill along the narrow street toward the parking lot on the far side of the piazza, the furthest cars were allowed to come into the historic center. Their backs were to the west, and the last light of day curved eastward, around their dark forms. They moved slowly, away from the edge of the gorge and the apartment, toward the center of town. A wind had risen, rushing through the corridors between the tight-set houses that bordered each side of the narrow street, and, as if the movement were choreographed, they both pulled their coats close around their necks. In the deepening gloom of twilight, neither of them spoke. At the front of the church, in the small piazza they passed through on their way, pigeons swooped overhead in one motion, like the stroke of a pen making a broad dark letter in the sky.

In front of the bakery adjoining the bar, at the entrance to the main piazza, Andrea, Silvio, and Giovanna were huddled in a compact circle, smoke from their cigarettes twirling wildly in the wind.

Leah barely knew the three of them. Silvio owned a knickknack store with Giulio, Andrea had the photo shop, and Giovanna, Silvio's girlfriend, appeared to be unemployed. Leah had seen her wandering through town, sometimes in the morning, other times in the afternoon.

Though they were all only acquaintances, Leah and Francesca, in the way of the town, stopped to say hello. It was a desultory greeting, slight nods of the head, the mandatory handshake, faces somber.

Leah regarded dark-eyed Giovanna. Her face was studded with heavy, metal piercings through her eyebrows, nose, and ears. She stood close beside Silvio, who was equally as "metaled" with a Mohawk haircut. The lanky, sloe-eyed Andrea stood a little to the side, the small but sullen distance a hint at his solitary character, a sign to the others that he preferred to guard his privacy.

The ritual of shaking hands befuddled Leah. She never got it right. Her father had taught her that a handshake should be firm, yet here it was more of a brushing of palms. She found it to be a vapid interchange, disconcerting given her own hardy character, because she could not feel the visceral spirit in such light touch of hands.

It was the two-cheek kiss that made her most at home, the closeness of faces, where the delicate grazing of cheeks revealed more friendship and warmth. But she was not close enough to these three for such a kiss, and she wasn't sure she wanted to be.

Silvio was the first to speak. His words flew upward on the wind, but then he raised his voice and Leah heard, ". . . a sad Befania."

Silvio's face was studded with thick silver earrings and two small silver bubbles joined by a shaft through the outer edge of his eyebrow. Sorting his features from the hardware, Leah saw that he was a handsome, small-boned man, of average height, with a high forehead, aquiline nose, and hands that gestured gracefully as he spoke. She could not imagine him in the Army, though she had heard he had been as a younger man. Now, his eyes glassy from drugs, he stood with his arms hanging loosely at his sides, leaning a little, as if resting his shoulder against an invisible wall.

Giovanna inclined toward him. Her long, slack hair wisped upward in the wind and twisted over her cheek. She brushed it back with short blunt fingers, though threads of it caught on her nose stud and she had to carefully unwind them before she tucked her hair over her ear, revealing large silver-hoop earrings, twins of Silvio's. Unlike her hair, her eyelashes were exceptionally long and thick, and Leah felt a pang of jealousy.

Giovanna's drug habit was new enough that though she too was glassy-eyed, her appearance did not detract from the powerful sensual pull that held both Silvio's and Andrea's attention.

For Leah, Andrea was the enigma. Average size like the rest, he was handsome in the way a person full of life is handsome. He had two loves, not counting what appeared to Leah to be his unreciprocated attraction to Giovanna: Music and old photos. When he sang, or spoke about his photos, his face took on light, an excitement infectious to those around him. Though his nose was askew on his face and his ears too large for his head, when he held his guitar, he brightened and became as handsome as any man Leah had ever seen. She had once watched him in the salon of the city offices playing for a town festival. His eyes glistened and danced like candlelight, and those listening, enthralled by his passion for the music, had gathered close around him, yearning to capture his intensity for their own spirits.

Still, no matter how subdued they appeared standing

here in the wind, wrapped in wild shrouds of smoke, Leah had lived in the town, for shorter or longer stays, enough to see all three of them furiously angry. In the dim light from the broad bakery windows, she studied their faces, wondering if, in anger, one of them could have shoved Giulio off the cliff, or if they were all simply prone to the normal protean Italian emotions.

"Umph." Andrea inclined his head, and then, strange to Leah, looked about them, as if to see if anyone were watching.

"What'er you looking for? Yesterday?" Giovanna poked Andrea in the ribs.

Andrea struck out with a backhand, which Giovanna missed only by a quick dodge to the right.

"My God, Andrea! What's the matter with you? I was only joking." She stepped away from him.

Andrea stared at her. His face was flushed with anger. "Don't fool with me, I'm not in the mood."

"You're never in the mood. All you think about are those lousy photos—and you won't even get them."

"As if you know. They're as good as mine right now."

"Well maybe Signora Seta will have something to say about it; even with Giulio gone she may decide to do something else."

"Shut up! Just shut up!"

She stepped forward and flipped her finger under his chin, then jumped back, huddling against Silvio. But Andrea did not respond.

Leah watched. It was as if Andrea had, in an instant,

deflated, and he stood now, head down, his arms at his sides.

Giovanna's voice trembled: "Some people have been saying we should cancel the Befania, but we're going ahead with it. Giulio would want us to. He loved the Befania, and if nothing else we should do it for him."

Silvio bristled. "Yeah, and you would know what Giulio wanted, wouldn't you!"

She tossed her head and glared at him. "Yes, as a matter of fact, I would."

Silvio threw his cigarette to the street and ground it back and forth with the toe of his muddy boot, as if it were a poisonous spider.

Watching the two of them Leah felt a strong desire to embrace them. She recognized a tinge of the tempestuous relationships of her youth, and if she were truthful with herself, of her marriage to Nick. She was still guilty of passionate jealousy and impetuous anger, yet she knew what a waste of passion and life those emotions were, and standing in the piazza, she was thankful that her daughter Sara was different than she was, than Silvio and Giovanna were being at the moment.

Andrea brought his hands together, palm to palm, shaking them up and down. "My God, Giulio's dead. He's dead. Let it go between the two of you, at least for tonight."

Silvio and Giovanna turned on him like snakes, and Silvio spat: "Oh, right. Just like you just let it go? Even if you don't, you should; you're closer to the photo collection than ever now, right?"

Andrea turned and stalked off.

Francesca pulled at Leah's coat sleeve, drawing her away, with a little wave at the group. "See you later."

Across the piazza, Leah leaned toward Francesca, "What was that all about?"

"Oh, I don't know. There's so much gossip. Let's talk about something else—your daughter's wedding. I don't want to even think about these sad things anymore."

But Leah did want to think about them.

Chapter Seven

Silvio and Giovanna watched the two women and Andrea walk away, then turned to each other.

"The two goody-goodies and the angry artist!" Silvio snarled.

"Yeah, Andrea is pretty touchy—I wonder why?"

"Because he had a big fight with fur coat today, that's why."

"Everybody has big fights with fur coat. That's nothing new."

"Then figure it out for yourself!"

"Talk about touchy! What's wrong with you? And why didn't you show up at our meeting spot today?"

"I had something else to do."

"Like what?"

"It's none of your business, damn it, lay off me."

Giovanna was quiet for a moment, her face reddening with anger. She lit a cigarette and bent to brush away a tattered wrapper that the wind had blown against her pant leg. As she bent, a necklace slipped out of her blouse, glittering in the light from the bar window.

"What's that?" Silvio asked, bending over to take hold of the necklace.

"Just a bauble." She straightened, reaching to pull it back from Silvio, but he clasped it firmly in his hand.

"It's not a bauble!" His face contorted into an ugly mask of jealousy. "It's Giulio's bullet. He's had it since we were in the Army together."

"So?"

"So what are you doing wearing it? It's his good luck charm."

"He gave it to me."

"When?"

"A while ago. What difference does it make? It's just an old bullet."

"If it's just an old bullet, then it doesn't matter to you, does it?"

He jerked the chain from around her neck and Giovanna toppled forward against him. With a swift snap of his arms he pushed her off.

"I knew it. I knew it. He stole my half of the drug money and he screwed around with my girl, and you"—Silvio's face contorted in fury—"you let him, you . . . so I'm right—and I gave him what he deserved."

There was a slice of pain at Giovanna's hairline and

she reached to feel along her neck. When she brought her hand up, she saw blood on her fingers from where the chain had cut her. At the same moment, she realized what Silvio had said.

"What do you mean, 'I gave him what he deserved?' Silvio, you didn't kill him did you? Is that why you didn't meet me?!"

Silvio shoved her away. "You fool. Shut your mouth. What do you think? Would I?"

The barber had stepped out from his shop just across the street and was staring at them. Silvio hurried away toward the smaller piazza below town.

"Lowlife! I could—" Giovanna yelled after him.

Silvio spun round. "You could what? Kill him? Kill me? Well Giulio's gone, but I'm still here, so just try whatever you want, fool!"

She watched him stomp away, waving the necklace, tight in his fist, punching the air above his head. Part of the chain had escaped from his hold and lashed back and forth with each movement of his arm. Digging in her pocket, she pulled out a tissue and lifted the hair off her neck so she could wipe away the blood. Anger and embarrassment whipped through her like a cloth in a strong wind, twisting and flapping, ready to be released.

The barber stepped toward her. "If I were you," he said, jabbing his finger at her, "I'd watch what I say these days."

"Up yours, you old goat." Giovanna strode down the darkened alley that led to her apartment. She would make up with Silvio; he would never relinquish his obsession for her, but she could not scrub her thoughts of her last meeting with Giulio.

They had been standing at the bottom of the back steps to town for the usual exchange of meth and money. For no reason she could understand, Giulio had told her he was cutting her off. When she protested, he tried to soothe her.

"Come on, Giovanna, it's for your own good. It's supposed to be fun, sweetie, but you're getting out of hand with it. And."—he hesistated—"I need my bullet back."

"It's supposed to be fun, sweetie," she mimicked. "I need my bullet back, sweetie, it's my little good luck charm . . ." Redfaced, she spat out the words. "You jerk, you're the one who started me on it. I pay you. You're the one who showed me what meth can do. You're the one who . . . never mind. But you'd better watch your back; one of us, one day, won't put up with it anymore."

She had egged her fear to anger and shouted at him: "You'll never get the bullet back!"

She shoved him hard against the wooden railing. The rotting pole, exposed to years of rain and humidity, broke and he went tumbling a few feet down into the thick brush of the hillside.

Seeing him fall, Giovanna turned and run up the steep trail to town. She heard him call her to come back, but she continued upward, panting hard, pounding the trail with her steps. Around a hairpin curve, she was startled to meet Secondo coming down. He opened his mouth to speak, but before he could she pushed by him and bolted upward to the steps that led her to the main street, where she rushed from bar to bar searching for that greasy-haired sleazeball Ottavio, the only other source she knew.

Remembering the incident with Giulio and then meeting Secondo, Giovanna relived the torment of not knowing if Secondo, from the trail above, had heard and seen the argument and if he had told anyone. She wondered, too, if anyone had seen her, early that morning of Giulio's death, tapping on his door, cursing the silence within as she shuddered against the early morning chill and her need.

Chapter Eight

Francesca guided the little green Fiat around the last curve and into the driveway. Tito, the sheep dog, rose and bounded to the length of his chain, which jerked his head back when he reached the end. As the car approached the house between the two stone columns of the gateway, he strained against the confines of the strong metal links.

Francesca turned to Leah with a little laugh. "It's as if he knows you're not a family member, isn't it? Even though to us you are."

Leah smiled, delighted to hear that she was considered family. She squeezed Francesca's arm, hoping the gesture conveyed with some eloquence what her fluid, but basic, Italian could not.

Sensitive to Leah's fear of the dog, Francesca pulled

the car forward at an angle away from Tito, until the bumper almost touched the south wall of the house.

Leah knew well to give Tito a wide berth. He was of old stock, a *Maremmana Abruzzese*, of aloof personality, and chillingly white, with a black nose and his tail set low. He had a deep, rounded ribcage that extended below his elbows, and he exuded a sense of horrible power. She treated the dog's dislike of her with good spirit, though each time she came to the farmhouse and heard his barking rip the air and saw him straining, muscle taut under fur against his chain, shivers ran up her spine.

Waist tall to Leah, she knew well that he was Leonardo's, a one-man/one-family dog, bred for the flocks, where he moved among the sheep as one of their own.

Though the flocks were gone, Tito's breeding still coursed through his veins, and it was only Leonardo's voice that could stop the dog's onslaught once he sensed a threat to his master or the family members.

The gravel crunched underfoot as they walked around the side of the house to the kitchen door. Across the drive, in the garden, the dusty-green leaves of the olive trees flickered in the gentle breeze and waning light. Below the trees, next to the walkway, the spiked spines of last year's artichoke plants spread in a ragged circle, one against the other.

Leah thought of summer, of the pasta Francesca's mother, Anna, served with fresh squash blossoms. She remembered the tomato sauce and bean soups she had eaten at the Antoninis' long dining room table, accompanied by wine from their grapes. She paused with her hand on the doorknob and gazed out over the small barn and the machine shed, out over the valley, bounded now, even in winter, by green hills and threaded by the Leora River. It was—it should be—idyllic, she thought.

Francesca waited behind Leah. A mature eighteen, she understood what Leah was seeing, and she, too, was thinking it should be idyllic, as it always had been for her. Giulio was one of her father's classmates at the high school. He was not a close friend, but she had known him since birth and had hoped to learn accordion from him so she could participate as a musician in the Befania.

Leah turned the knob, and she and Francesca entered the welcome heat of the kitchen.

Inside, Francesca's mother, Anna, and her maternal grandmother, Rosetta, were scuttling about the kitchen, while Francesca's paternal grandmother, Carla, stood to the side, leaning against the door frame, watching. Her apron was dusted with flour, and having just rinsed her hands after kneading the dough that was now rising at the back of the counter, she was drying her fingers and palms carefully with a small yellow hand towel. The heavy iron wood-stove, which sat tight against the gas one, was pouring out heat.

Seeing Leah, Anna set the pizza she had just retrieved

from the oven on the marble worktable in the center of the room and embraced the younger woman with the sides of her arms, keeping her flour-dusted hands at a distance. They kissed each other delicately on both cheeks.

"Leah." She said the name with a gentle affection and backed off, opening her arms, to display herself. "I'm hot and sweaty."

Sprinkles of flour mottled her clothes, and her cheeks shone bright red. Leah smiled and stepped close to give Anna a real hug, disregarding the flour. "Hot and sweaty doesn't bother me!"

They both laughed. Leah loved this beautiful, strong woman. Anna's no–nonsense spirit and joy surfaced in her eyes and gave her skin an aura of goodwill.

"So many pizzas!"

"Oh, just little ones."

Francesca piped up from the doorway. "Wait. You'll see the desserts in the other room. And my mother made them all!"

Leah stepped to the table and counted the square pizzas. "Ten of them. They're beautiful."

"Plain. But it's what people like, just dough and tomato sauce—and of course a few white ones as well." Anna turned to put another pizza in the oven.

Leah and Anna were the same height, just over five feet, but Anna was of stronger build, with long straight brown hair pulled back, unlike Leah's own loose curls.

Anna's cheeks glowed from the heat in the kitchen and from the wind and sun of the olive grove and garden. Her hands showed the veins and thick fingers of a woman accustomed to hard work. Leah knew that when Anna hugged her, she meant it; the welcome was always genuine.

She also knew that Anna would never hug her or invite her if she weren't welcome. Generous to the bone, joyous in company and in her work, she was impatient with foolishness, quick to perceive falsehood, and willing to speak her keen mind on any subject from friendship to politics. But the best part was her laughter and her insistent urging for Leonardo to tell another of his jokes, especially those about the the national police.

Leah remembered several of the police jokes, and looking at the woman in front of her, recalled one from the last time she had eaten with the Antoninis. They had laughed long and hard when Leonardo told the joke. He was a gifted storyteller, but now, at the memory of it, only a slight smile grazed Leah's lips. The laughter was gone for now.

Leah regarded Anna, whose strength and grace reminded Leah of her own midwestern farm upbringing. Like the farm women Leah had grown up with, Anna was inured to hard work. She could prune their olive trees, help butcher, and on the same day, serve a dinner of thick, homemade bean soup, roast lamb, oven potatoes with rosemary, green salad, and torte. Leah had once read that "hard work spotlights the character of people" and she saw it was true with Anna, whose every act was for the good of her family.

While Leonardo was away in the city, working as an engineer, Anna labored on the farm with the help of her mother, Rosetta. In her characteristic stance, the older woman crossed her arms and cupped her elbows in her palms. She watched the interchange between her daughter and Leah, waiting until she deemed it appropriate to step forward and hug Leah with an embrace equally as genuine as Anna's.

After she had kissed Leah on both cheeks, Rosetta grasped Leah's shoulders and looked straight into her eyes.

"Leah."

It was all she said, one word in a voice that bespoke pure friendship and commiseration over the recent losses to cancer of Rosetta's husband and Leah's own mother.

Dressed always in a long skirt and knitted top, graying hair closely clipped and her eyeglasses sliding down her nose, Rosetta rarely spoke. She had the same build as Anna. Since her husband, Ugo, had died, she teared in emotional moments, but nothing stopped her from working the farm on which she and Ugo had lived all their married life. Like her own mother, Rosetta was a farm wife, accustomed to trimming the vines, planting, and harvesting the garden, butchering, and cleaning. She had taught Anna the same work, carried out with the same quiet joy. Now, even as the years passed and she had arrived at her mid-seventies, she worked alongside her daughter at every job, matching the younger woman's pace.

Carla, Leonardo's mother, came to hug Leah last, stepping forward from where she had been standing on the opposite side of the kitchen leaning against the lintel with her hands clasped. She was the grandmother from town; frustrated by macular degeneration, she helped as she could.

Her gift, Leah had learned, was telling stories. And this she did with care and an acute attention to detail. At every meal she recounted one memory or another of the town when she was young, teaching Francesca the history of the place. A thin, frail woman, her hands moved constantly. As her stories unraveled, she straightened or brushed crumbs from the table cloth, picked a bit of lint from Francesca's shoulder, or rubbed one hand over the other as they lay in her lap. Leah imagined that she might be driven to this restlessness by the sadness of the loss of her husband.

In her early eighties, her memory was keen. Leah remembered how she recalled the incident of World War I, when the women and children had made a procession out of town, down the steep hillside, across the bridge spanning the Lavini River and up the rough dirt roadway toward the Church of Santa Maria to pray for their husbands, fathers, and brothers.

As they passed under the sheer tufa wall below the

church, the rock face had given way. Huge boulders rumbled onto the procession in a thick river of rock, crushing fifty-one women and children before cascading into the valley below. The screams of the mothers and wives and children had been lost in the thunder of the rock downpour.

Telling it, Carla brought her hand to her mouth, covering her lips, shaking her head slowly from side to side.

"That's the reason for the cross and those columns that rise up from the tangle of vines and brush there at the roadside. Almost everyone has forgotten, but I remember, and the other ones my age remember."

She paused.

"It was as bad as when the Americans bombed the piazza and killed ninety-one of us. But they didn't mean to. The bomb went astray."

At the end of the story, she had shaken her head slowly, whisking bread crumbs from the table with one smooth white hand into the palm of the other.

Chapter Nine

Francesca took Leah by the arm. "Enough sadness for now. Come to the living room and see the pastries."

Leah turned to Anna with a questioning look. Anna patted her shoulder. "I know you want to hear about Giulio. It's been a shock to all of us, but Leonardo will tell you about it later. Go with Francesca for now. See the food for the Befania and take some pictures for your husband's research."

The living room initially had been the family cantina, with great barrels of wine on a raised portion of the floor, and sausages and prosciutto hanging from the ceiling. But when Ugo had fallen ill, Leonardo and Anna had renovated the room, and added, as well, a back bedroom and bath behind the living room so

69

that Ugo and Rosetta could be on the ground floor. Now, a breakfront stood at the far end of the room, away from the double-door entryway, through which the various groups of the Befania would enter, group by group as they made their rounds throughout the night.

A wide, cherry-wood structure with a middle counter between two cabinets, the breakfront was laden not only with desserts, but with deviled eggs topped with a swirl of red and white mayonnaise and a bit of black olive, with dishes of home cured olives from the Antoninis' own trees, and with the uncured Tuscan salami, *soprasatta*. Francesca had arranged the desserts at the far end of the counter. Leah pointed at the first, long rectangular pieces of brittle pastry, covered with powdered sugar. "What's this one?"

"It's called *cenci* or *frappe*. We always have them for the Befania."

"And this?"

"*Crostata di ricotta*. We call it alcamese, And those two," she pointed, "are crostate as well, apple and another ricotta, but not sweet."

"And that big rectangular cake? The one covered with hundreds and thousands?"

"Hundreds and thousands?"

Leah laughed. "The colored sprinkles. I just translated it directly from English. I don't know the Italian word for them."

Now Francesca laughed. "I don't know what we call them either. The cake is *ricciolma*. It's very very good."

"Ah! *Castagnole*." Leah took one of the golden brown round balls of pastry that was covered with powdered sugar and raised it to her mouth, then, embarrassed, stopped herself, hesitant to put it back because she had touched it. "Sorry! I didn't even think. They just looked so good."

Francesca laughed again. "Eat, Leah. Eat. That's what they're for."

Leah popped the sweet ball of dough into her mouth.

"Mamma!" Francesca called into the other room, laughing. "Leah can't stop herself. She's eating the castagnole."

Anna's voice carried a lilt of laughter. "Good! It will put a little meat on her bones. Tell her to have a sciace as well."

Leah looked at Francesca, puzzled. "Does she mean foccacia?"

"That's what *you* call it."

Just as Leah walked into the kitchen smiling, a half-eaten castagnole in her hand, Leonardo opened the kitchen door and stepped inside. Leah noted his haggard look, though his features still reflected a genuine and gentle concern for his family as he nodded in greeting to them.

"Hello, Leah." He reached to take her hand, and

smiled when she transferred the castagnole to her left hand, wiping her right hand on her jeans before she extended her arm.

Leonardo epitomized gentility and kindness, with no accompanying sense of weakness or lack of resolve. Like his wife, he exuded integrity, and as she clasped his hand Leah felt again the great gift of having him and his family for friends.

"I'm sorry about Giulio. I know it's been a shock."

"Yes, a shock." He nodded and passed his hand over his face as if to erase the memory of Giulio clawing the air as he fell to earth. "Well, we'll talk about it later. I think I need to get cleaned up, no?" He had turned to Anna; there was a brief glance between the two of them, but Anna answered only, "Yes."

Chapter Ten

They were all quiet as they sat around the long table in the dining room. Leah glanced at each one in turn. The trauma of the day had heightened her senses and made her yet more intensely aware of their genuine humility, their grace without affectation. It was the sort of manner that brooked no untruth, but expressed truths and opinions in a thoughtfully open and straightforward way not tinged by pretense or catty criticism. It was the opposite of murder. She could trust them; she teetered on the edge of revealing what she had seen. Mistaken perhaps as her decision was, and poorly reasoned, she knew Leonardo had seen Giulio fall to his death and she could not bring herself to introduce more pain or the terror of her own experience into this household. Soon the Befania would begin and throughout the night, group after group would be approaching the house, each one led by a man or a couple or a threesome dressed in exaggerated women's dress, with a partner—man or woman—in men's clothes, and a daughter dressed the same: A jumble of scarves and skirts. The members of the group would sing as they approached, and once inside, would dance, eat, and drink with the hosts in the sweet ritual of exchange that recalled the traditional, dignified gift of food from farmers like Leonardo and Anna to the poor of the countryside. The groups coming from other areas would know nothing of Giulio or his death, and it would be enough for Anna and Leonardo to host each group under the weight of sadness, without worry for her.

After the soup, as they were eating the main course, speaking in a near whisper Leonardo began the story of what he had seen. His handsome, weathered face was tense with emotion and with effort, but his voice, by force of will, remained steady. Though not a close friend, he had been a classmate of Giulio's. The town was small, and the two often saw each other and spoke about friends and weather, and particularly about hunting.

Leah sensed that it was not only the death of Giulio that caused the pained expression on Leonardo's face, but the damage the community had sustained—the suspicion and terror it created among the townspeople.

"I was hunting along the river, just below the bench. A few days ago, I had run into Giulio in town, and he told me he'd seen cinghiale in that spot a few days before. He was excited about going hunting and was planning to go out himself later in the day. He seemed happier than he'd been lately; he said his aunt had been talking to him about the cantina she has on the north side of town, below the church. She told him he was going to inherit it, and he was glad to know that because he thought she was giving it to Andrea.

"Anyway, since I had the next day off as well, I called the police when I got home and asked them if I could bring my gun in the car to that area, and they gave me permission."

Leah looked puzzled.

He nodded his head toward her, his dark eyes intent and his high forehead glistening with perspiration in the light. "It's the law here, Leah. We have to ask. It's not like America." A slight smile crossed his lips.

She nodded, curious to ask him more about the law, but unwilling to interrupt the story, and Leonardo continued, the soft "shh" sound of the Tuscan dialect more pronounced than usual.

"I was bushwhacking with Tito along the river, upstream, when I heard the scream. I looked up—I had to shade my eyes against the glare of the sun—and I saw a man flailing in the air. I didn't know then, of course, that it was Giulio. It seemed as if the falling would never end, and yet at the same time it was happening too quickly, and there was nothing I could do.

"I was standing about thirty feet from where he fell. It was a feeling of impotence. Like I said, I didn't realize it was Giulio, but the blue coveralls looked familiar, and I knew it must be someone from around here, and I couldn't do anything.

"He crashed through the limbs of the trees; the branches cracked and broke, and then he hit with a terrible thud. Tito ran for him, and when I reached him, Tito was standing beside him, sniffing. I couldn't yet see the face, but I knew by his posture that he was already dead.

"His legs and arms were askew and he was cut and bleeding, but the worst was the way his neck tilted to one side, like a bird that had hit a window.

"I called the police on my cell phone, and I'm glad I had it with me because I didn't want to leave him alone, and I was lucky I made the call when I did, because when I edged around to the other side of the body, I saw it was Giulio, and I dropped the phone and after it wouldn't work. All I could think was how happy Giulio had been about the cantina the day before, and about how, when we were kids together, he was always singing, like he sings for the Befania.

"When the lieutenant and Sergeant Gianicollo got there, I was surprised that they paid little attention to the body. They had told me on the phone to step away from it and not to touch anything, so I called Tito back to me and we stood there waiting, just looking at Giulio. I suppose it's their job to think of crime, but to me it seemed a cold—even if necessary—way to handle it.

"They stretched tape in a circle around the area, and Gianicollo took pictures with his little digital camera . . ."

Leah moved uneasily in her chair, her face flushed a bright red as everyone looked toward her.

"I'm sorry Leah, I'm upsetting you? Shall I stop?"

"No. No. Please go ahead." She plucked at the sleeve of her sweater, and shrugged out of it, twisting to drape it over the back of her chair. She felt a sharp stab of guilt and was tempted again to tell the Antoninis what she knew. The others looked at her, and Francesca rose and moved around the table to open the front door a crack so the cold air could flow in. Leonardo continued.

"It was something about the way Giulio had fallen, or where he had fallen, that made them think he hadn't jumped, but that it was murder."

Leonardo fell silent, his head lowered.

"I told them Giulio never would have jumped. Never. He was cantankerous, a fighter, generous to the core, impetuously so, even. Unfortunately, he got into drugs once he was out of the Army. Still, he was stubborn, he always thought himself in the right. I used to argue with him over so many little things . . ."

Leonardo smiled at the memory.

". . . but it was his character to be obstinate like that, and he never got depressed enough to do away with himself, even with the drugs."

Leah squirmed again in her seat and reached for the plate of asparagus to cover her discomfort. "Who do you think could have killed him?"

The question was so straightforward and unexpected that Leonardo emitted a cough, as if someone had struck him on the back. He reached for his glass of water, and took a long drink before he set the glass back on the table.

"This is the most difficult for us. We can't think of who would have done this. Who from our town would have done this?!"

She realized she was being typically American: Blunt, impolitic, maybe even impolite, but she could not stop herself from pressing on. "Maybe he's not from here. It's possible, no?"

"What? A tourist?" He raised his eyebrows and hunched his shoulders.

"I–I don't know. We can't know, right?" She tried to cover her embarrassment. "Maybe someone from Visula?"

"No, we know those people almost as well as the people here. And Giulio? Who would want to kill Giulio? And what for?"

Carla interjected. "And no one knows where Giulio's Aunt Luisa is. They can't find her. She told me she planned to go to the coast to meet a friend from Rome, but she didn't say who it was or where they were staying, or even if they are staying on the coast. It's terrible that she doesn't yet know and we all do. She'll be traumatized." She brushed at her skirt as if to dust off crumbs.

"Did you tell the police, Nonna?" Francesca turned to her grandmother.

"No police to tell. I asked, but one was out with the body and like Leonardo said, the other one has gone to the provincial office, and with the road like it is after the storm, all torn up, and the lines down, he'll be gone a long while."

Chapter Eleven

"Me? I never hunt cinghiale in the day—or under the full moon." Italo glanced at Nick for what seemed to Nick the hundredth time, and Nick silently cursed the fact that there had been no room in one of the other cars.

When Italo took a curve at full speed, swinging into the other lane and narrowly missing an oncoming car, the driver of the other car laid on the horn, but Italo appeared not to notice.

"During the day, or with the light of the moon— that's baby stuff. I wait until it's a moonless night. And I never shoot until I am as close to the boar as I am to you now. If you looked in my trunk you could see my rifle; it's a beauty."

"I thought I heard you can't carry guns in the car?"

"That law's for sissies!"

Nick grimaced. He wondered who Italo's friends were. The others who had met for the Befania all appeared to know him, and Nick had seen him often in Scansansiano, but knew from the talk that Italo didn't live there. A handsome man with green eyes and wispy, dark blond hair, Italo was generous in the way of buying drinks and treating people to meals, though few accepted his offers because his bragging gave them headaches, as it was giving Nick at the moment. Suffering the drone of Italo's voice, Nick could understand why he was tolerated and not befriended. Nick remembered seeing him dance once in the bar and was reminded of the professional dancers on American TV: One felt a superficial, instantaneous allurement, but once out of sight, once the TV was turned off, they were forgotten until the next time they twirled across the screen.

Italo's girlfriend Angelina, a woman of uncertain age—Nick thought not more than twenty-five at most and maybe younger—also befuddled Nick. Before they had started from town, while they stood in the piazza waiting for the others, he had been talking with her, surprised by her strident voice as well as her looks. A tall woman, Nick thought that most people would consider her unattractive because of her deeply pockmarked face. To him, her wide set eyes, acquiline nose, and wide lips held a rough physical attraction. Still, she was the opposite of what Nick thought Italo would have chosen. As he spoke with her, he realized, it was not the pockmarks that would distance people from her, it was her contrary attitude, and Nick began to wonder how Italo could stand being around her for long. When he had suggested to her that it might rain, she countered with certainty that it would not. When he expressed his excitement about the evening's events, she suggested that something would probably go wrong.

Yet, disagreeing with everything he said, she wouldn't let him go, clinging to the conversation as if it were food to a starving person. She pushed him away and yet wanted to keep him, and more, it felt as if she were trying to pry information from him.

"Where's your wife? What work does she do? Do you have children?"

He had to remind himself to be generous; she had explained to him how the Befania couple, the Befano and the Befana, prepared by disguising themselves in advance in early era clothes, rubber masks, and heavy makeup. Still, when he saw the others stepping into the cars, he was glad to interrupt her with a hurried, "I better go or I'll be left behind," and scuttle off to Andrea's car.

To Nick's suprise, the first farmhouse was close to the road and was newly built. Tumbling out of the cars, the motley members of the group drifted toward the house, singly and in pairs, singing the traditional song, one but separate, their voices preceding them into the night air. Nick was suprised at the huge picture windows facing the south, an American innovation. A wide stairway led to the second story, where the family's main rooms were located, and forming a tight group, they squeezed into the width of the stairway and clambered together up the travertine steps.

No one came to the porch to meet them. The owner of the house stood in the doorway, ushering them in to the large sitting room in a haughty, peremptory manner uncharacteristic of local hospitality. Inside, the high white walls were laden with pretentious paintings, and two poorly executed sculptures of draped, kneeling women stood in opposite corners at the far end of the room. Three small plates of store-bought cookies had been haphazardly placed on one edge of the table near the doorway, and there were two inexpensive store-bought bottles of wine.

The family and their friends gathered at one end of the room, away from the table, leaving their guests to chat amongst themselves at the other end. Without even a tap of their feet to the music, family members watched the initial dance of Befano and Befana, as if observing a play on stage. Seeing this, Andrea picked up the tempo, playing a little louder, hoping it would incite the family to participate, to take joy in the tradition, and make a special effort—though he was uncertain if they knew about Giulio. The accordion weighed against his chest and he was sweating profusely, but his efforts were fruitless; the family remained distant. Silvio slowly walked the length of the room and pleaded with the wife of the household to dance the traditional Befano and hostess dance with him, but rather than dancing herself, she pushed her daughter forward. After much cajoling, the daughter reluctantly agreed, though as the last note sounded, she turned and rushed back to the end of the room to her parents and friends.

The Befania troupe absorbed the chill of the atmosphere. Nick had moved off to a corner, away from Italo.

The others were speaking to each other quietly, with little enthusiasm, but when Andrea muttered something about missing Giulio, Italo snapped in a voice that carried throughout the room. "I bet you're glad. You were next in line to inherit the cantina and the collection of old photos from his aunt. And even if you don't care as much about the cantina, you wanted those photos. They must be worth hundreds of millions of lira."

"You shut up. You don't know anything about it! And it's you who cares so much; you knew Giulio wouldn't have sold you the cantina for your precious restaurant." Andrea raised his hand as if to strike Italo, then lowered his fist with an act of will, spun on his heel, and stormed out of the door.

The room fell quiet, except for titters from the daughter and her friends. The husband of the family hesitated, watching, and then rose, walked to the doorway and stood, issuing by his stance and hand on the door handle, a silent, cold invitation for the troupe to leave. Slowly, led by Silvio, they filed through the door and followed

Andrea down the steps and across the grassy expanse of yard toward the cars.

Italo came from near the coast, and from what he said, Nick understood that he usually came to town only for holidays. When Leonardo had first introduced Nick to Italo in the broad expanse of the piazza, Italo seemed a friendly, talented talker. He described in detail to Nick his farm near the coast and his business in car sales for Fiat. His Italian was clear and educated, and sadly, Nick thought, without a trace of the local dialect. But the idea of an interesting discussion about the Befania was quickly dispelled: Now back in the car, without prelude, Italo had bolted into a tirade of gossip about the town and the locals.

"I couldn't live here. People here don't understand business. They have no ambition. Tradition, yes; ambition, no. And people *would* come here—and pay—for that tradition. But these bumpkins don't know it; or if they do know it, they don't know what to do about it. If there were a good, I mean really good, restaurant, they would come from Rome and Florence just to eat here."

Nick protested. "But there are good restaurants here—and people *do* come from Rome and Florence on the weekends."

"I mean *people* . . . important people. Like the ones my friend works with in the ministry, the upper echelons, you know?"

"Angelina works in the ministry? I thought she was in real estate."

"She is, but she also does some secretarial work for one of the ministers."

"She's your girlfriend, right?"

"Well, you could call her that, but my wife and kids wouldn't like it." He laughed at his own wit.

"Your wife and kids?" Nick coughed.

"Of course I have a family . . ."

"But what about your wife?"

"She does as I tell her. Besides, she knows Angelina."

"This is incredible. And she—"

"And nothing. She's full of hot air." Italo imitated his wife: " 'You keep her away from here, from our family and friends or I'll kill her!' But she won't. She's a little mosquito; she buzzes and she irritates, but she doesn't kill."

"Does Angelina know about her and the kids?"

"I just told you. Of course. They know each other. They went to school together. And when she's angry, Angelina says the same thing as Sofia, 'I'll kill her!' But she won't kill her because they went to school together and their families know each other, and besides, she likes Sofia."

Italo hesistated. "But of course, Angelina is more of a wasp than a mosquito. You do pay for love with pain that's for sure, and there isn't any love without jealousy. If it were anybody but Sofia!"

"I think maybe you don't know women as well as

you think you do. What if the mosquito and the wasp join forces?"

Italo laughed. "Be calm, Nick. They're not going to and neither one of them is going to hurt the other. They're both devoted, and really, both of them are gentle and loving."

Surprised at the sudden tenderness in Italo's voice, Nick saw that relieved of bravado, Italo's features regained a handsome outline and smooth forehead. *What a little boy, what a fool.* Nick thought. *What a fool.* And then he caught himself wondering if the stereotype about Italian men and their mistresses were true.

"Listen Nick, Angelina is . . . well, she is devoted to me." The devil had came back in his eyes. "I think she would lick my boots if I asked her—and maybe . . ." He laughed crudely and reaching over, punched Nick in the arm.

Nick let it go, resigned to his fate, and they rode in silence. As boring and unpleasant as Italo seemed, Nick guessed he must be a successful businessman, by the way he spoke and because he wore a subtle but expensive dark green suit cut and tailored in the dress style of the old Roy Rogers films from the 1950s.

Italo broke Nick's musings as if there had been no hiatus in the conversation.

"She'll be along tomorrow night; I saw you two talking."

"Angelina? Yes, she said something about real estate business in town."

"And that's not what she's best at, if you get what I mean!" Italo's face contorted with an ugly grin. "She's nuts. Her dad is always beating her and she likes the rough stuff." He laughed. "But hey, she also thinks I'm a god, and should have whatever I want, so who's complaining?" Excited, he worked his hands back and forth on the steering wheel.

"She's being abused *now*?"

"Oh, god yes. Her dad beats her every chance he gets."

"But—"

"You mean, why doesn't somebody do something about it?"

"Yeah."

"Everybody knows it, and we've all talked to her about it, but she won't press charges and she won't move out."

"Why?"

"Who knows? It's her business." He shrugged and leaned into the door as he took another curve.

They followed the other members of the group in the cars ahead, down State Road 102, the same narrow winding asphalt road Leah had taken earlier with Francesca. Italo had reverted to talking about his exploits hunting cinghiale, and Nick willed himself to enjoy this night, this man's company, because no matter how crude he was, he was a folklorist's dream as a storyteller.

This was the way of fieldwork. Ninety percent of the

time you struggled through useless conversations, or worse, knowing you wouldn't use what you heard, and wishing you hadn't heard parts of it. But then there was the 10 percent of the conversations that made up for it all, so Nick persisted, hoping for the 10 percent.

"It must be scary. Those tusks are serious."

"No, no. Most of them just run away. And I never hunt those. They're the dumb ones. I only want to hunt the intelligent, brave ones. I'm not like the people around here who just go out to get the meat. They don't understand the sport of it, the challenge. You have to put yourself on an equal footing, 'even the odds' is how you say it, right?"

He emitted a loud guffaw, proud of his self-proclaimed prowess and for knowing the English term. "It's not for nothing that in this part of Tuscany we have PMSB on our regional flag."

"PMSB?"

"Poverty, malaria, sweat, and blood. A hard life that produces hard men. Blood, Nick, blood." He straightened his shoulders, demonstrating that he was one of the hard men.

Nick grunted. "Well, I suppose it's important to get the meat too, isn't it?"

"Of course, of course, but it's not the ultimate goal; it doesn't show the ancient, courageous spirit of hunting—and I can't stand hunting with someone who doesn't want it dangerous. It's the same in business. I hate wimps. If you're in business you have to go at it like a hunt. Just what the people around here don't do. Like

Giulio, not to speak ill of the dead, but he was a pansy. He could have gotten his aunt to stop waffling on that cantina and sign it over to him long ago, but he didn't press her on it."

Nick thought of pansies he had seen, braving the snow, blossoming against the white. "But what difference does it make to you?"

Italo suddenly turned angry. "Oh nothing! Forget it! It's better this way anyway."

"What's better?"

Italo tried to laugh it off. "Forget it. Take a look in the back seat." He poked his thumb over his shoulder.

Nick turned.

"See that hat?

"Yeah. It looks like one of our fancy western cowboy hats."

"No. One of *our* cowboy hats. Much, much better than yours, and way more expensive. An *Italian* cowboy hat. You know about the Italian cowboys don't you?"

"Of course—"

"Well"—petulant once again, Italo interrupted—"I'm a cowboy."

"I thought you worked for Fiat."

"I do." He scowled at Nick. "But I'm really a cowboy. And my grandfather was as well. You may know a little, Nick, but you don't know it all. We were the ones who beat Buffalo Bill when he came here in the 1880s. He thought he'd just walk in and show up the local yokels! But we showed him." Italo rubbed his hands on the steering wheel again in agitation. "Anyway, that hat cost me hundreds of lira. Hundreds! And I can afford it because I don't wait around like some people." He was grinding his teeth. "I go after what I want."

Following an increasingly irrational path, Italo's diatribe created a tingling of fear up Nick's arms and across his back. Considering Italo's obsession with his own courage and abilities, his bravado about starting a new restaurant in Scansansiano, and the way he had denigrated Giulio's business acumen, Nick wondered if this smart-looking blowhard beside him was capable of murdering someone to get what he wanted. He decided to change the subject to avert Italo's attention.

"Wasn't too lively at that last house, was it?"

"Those people are just showoffs. They think they're above everyone else. Such jerks. And Andrea. Phew! I said that stuff about him because it's true. He wants those photos so bad he can taste it. Did you see how he stormed out? But forget it, I should have kept quiet. Andrea and I have never been friends. But tonight it was that house—they're cold fish, those people. A generation ago, they were street sweepers in Rome, and now with the money their grandfather left them, they're landowners. We say 'Arrogance goes by horse and comes back by foot.'"

Nick sneezed to cover his own burst of laughter. He wondered when Italo would be coming back by foot.

Oblivious, Italo rushed on. "They're Romans! They don't know anything about the tradition of the Befania around here. For them it's just stupid dolls imported from China that are made to look not like our Befana, but like your American Halloween witches. They go for an evening walk in Piazza Navonna, all lit up for Epiphany, buy a cheap doll and tell the kids it's the Befana. And besides, if they had fed us better tonight, nothing would have happened."

"*Around here?* I thought *you* weren't from around here."

Italo ignored him and switched subject. "Say, have you heard the story of Tiburzi?" He poked Nick in the shoulder. "You should have, in your line of work."

"Yes, I've heard it."

"But you've only heard the official story. The one they tell in all those stupid tourist books. Am I right?"

"That's right."

Nick tilted his head back against the seat, hoping the coming story would be as good as others Italo had told. As they took yet another curve at high speed, Nick grasped the door handle. On the other side of the window the edges of the forests whipped by in the car's head-lights. In front of them were the other four cars, and Nick wished again that he had been able to squeeze into Andrea's car with the bigger group even though he was about to hear about Tiburzi. He wondered how Leah was doing; if she was holding up under the strain of silence.

Suddenly, Italo broke into song, startling Nick, who jerked under his seat belt.

"I will sing of the noble brigand
that one day ruled this land
was named King of the Maremma
and for thirty years his reign endured

He made the hearts of men tremble
And gave bread to those in need
Domenico Tiburzi was his name
And in the sad and moonless night
With his rifle strapped across his chest
He defied storms and luck."

Here, Italo interrupted himself. "The song is too long for me to sing the whole thing, so I'll skip to the last stanzas where it tells of his death and his very odd burial. Listen."

"They say that one night at Farene
While he was happy with his friends
There was an ambush and he couldn't save himself.

Like this he was carried to sacred earth
Where he was buried half-in and half-out of the
    cemetery
Half in consecrated ground, half in the eternity of
    hell."

Italo held the last note, then laughed with a great roar and stepped on the accelerator.

"He *did* have a strange burial, half-in and half-out of the cemetery, half sacred in heaven and half damned in hell. But if it wasn't Capitano Michele Giacheri who killed him in those bushes outside the little hideout in Farene, then who was it?" Italo asked rhetorically. "He killed himself! He had way too much courage and dignity to let himself be killed by a local policeman. Way too much. My great-grandfather knew him. And I don't mean 'knew of him' I mean *knew* him—and he said Tiburzi was too proud to ever die at the hand of anyone else."

Nick shook his head; Italo's voice was truly exquisite. No matter how crude he was, he was an ideal informant and Nick promised himself he would interview him at length once the murderer was in jail and Leah was safe.

"What you're saying makes me think of poor Giulio. I wonder if maybe he killed himself?"

"Poor Giulio?" Italo grunted. "Could be. Giulio was a loser. He had no drive; he just wanted to sing and wait for his inheritance from his aunt."

"That's what you were talking about? The cantina? The photos?"

"Initially it was to go to Andrea because Giulio and his aunt had a big argument, but then Giulio and his aunt made up. That's why I said that to Andrea. I heard it from a pretty good source."

"Like?"

"Never mind. Who wants to waste time with those

jokers, anyway? Tiburzi was in another whole class. A man who knew what he wanted and wasn't afraid to go for it."

With an effort strengthened by the habit of interviewing informants, Nick followed Italo's lead and proposed another open-ended question so maybe he would come back round to Giulio. "That's a great story. How did your grandfather know him?"

"Great-grandfather. History, Nick. History, not 'stories.' Everybody around there knew him, but my great-grandfather played cards with him. Tiburzi was like the English Robin Hood, but he was craftier. Picky. He knew who to please and how to stay alive by being in the good graces of people who mattered. And he never would have let Giacheri get him. He was the last of the ancient Etruscans, living by a different code."

Italo said it as if he were speaking about himself.

"And when Italy decided to unify, I guess it was just the end of an era and time for him to go. When we have more time, I'll tell you the whole story. You can record me. I'm a good talker, aren't I?" He turned and grinned at Nick.

In the dim light of the interior of the car, Nick was silent, remembering a proverb: Pride eats breakfast with plenty, dines with poverty, and sups with shame.

Nearing the Leora River, Italo slowed the car and took a left turn following the others up a dirt road that must at one time have been a via cava. Nick noted the murky mouths of caves as they drove along, winding through the steep, tree-topped walls toward the ridge.

A few days before, Andrea had told him this would be a "magical" night. He had said the word repeatedly, excitedly, wonderfully enthusiastic, Nick thought, for his own traditions—so much so that Nick had been infected by his exuberance. The arrogant ones were all part of it, he reminded himself, hoping the trip would not be a total bust.

It was not.

Out of the cars, the group strolled toward the door. Terzo, whom Nick had seen working in the electrician's shop, was ringing a cowbell to announce their arrival, Andrea and Angelo, a young man who worked in the small grocery story just off the piazza in town, were playing their accordions, and the butcher, Giovanni, was strumming his guitar. All of them sang the traditional approach song:

> *"Good evening everyone*
> *Tonight is the Befania*
> *And in the name of Mary*
> *We come to greet you . . ."*

As soon as he had stepped out of the car, Nick punched the record button on his tape recorder and was catching the song and the troupe's feet crunching on gravel. His recorder was slung over his neck, the microphone mounted on a little metal arm that stuck out three inches from his chest. He held the camera that Leah had given him years ago and moved around and among the group, snapping photos as they sang, bunched together at the doorway. The farmers welcomed them, stepping out, smiling, listening with pleasure to the singing, and as the last stanza faded, they parted to welcome their guests into the house.

Inside, Nick had a flash of understanding of what the Befania must have been like in decades—and perhaps centuries—past. Around the darkened, low-ceilinged room the family and their other guests—almost all older people dressed in the traditional black of the peasants—welcomed them with typical humble quietness. In one corner, a wood-burning stove cast a welcome heat, and beside it, a long trestle table was laden with homemade cakes, sausages, wine, cheeses, sandwiches of tuna pate, and biscotti.

But before anyone moved to the food, the Befano and the Befana stretched their arms toward each other for the first dance, while the rest of the group and the hosts and their friends gathered round to watch. The sounds of the musicians' instruments and their rich voices filled the room as the couple danced in wild and raucous circles, twirling from side to side like dolls given life.

As Nick regarded the Befana and Befano dancing and the others standing along the walls, he was suprised to see Secondo sitting amongst the family members. Secondo was what he thought of as the town orphan, although the man was thirty-four years old. As he watched him sip his wine, Nick made a note to himself to research the naming practice of calling children ordinal numbers. The odd thing, Nick thought, was that Leonardo had told Nick that Secondo was an only child; there was no Primo.

From the local gossip, Nick had learned that Secondo had mental problems, and, as nearly as he could tell, it was bipolar illness. His father had committed suicide when Secondo was little, and his mother had cared for Secondo by herself through various episodes, until she had died just after Secondo's thirty-second birthday. Nick had spoken with him in the bar a few times, and he had seemed perfectly normal, but Nick had also seen him unshaven and dirty wandering the town, singing at the top of his voice, running from one store to another to chatter incessantly at townspeople in the piazza.

Once he had learned about Secondo's problems, Nick had made it a habit on early Saturday mornings to leave a roll of lira in the mailbox of the tiny apartment where Secondo lived alone. The barmaid, Sabina, had told Nick that Secondo had the apartment, but that she often saw him sleeping on one bench or another, even in the winter, when she walked home from her late shift at the bar. She, like the others, assumed it was his illness that drove him out of doors, but she had failed to recognize that his night forays had only begun since his mother died.

Secondo saw Nick watching him and waved. Nick waved back, happy to see him enjoying the Befania, with a plate of food balanced on his lap and aglass of wine firmly in his grasp. But in the same instant, the dark thought that Secondo, in one of his episodes, was capable of murder flitted through his mind.

The host and his wife, their eyes glittering with pleasure, had danced with the Befano and the Befana. The music over, they came to Nick with a glass of their own wine and a tray of cheeses and cakes.

"American?" the wife asked.

"Yes." Nick smiled at her and her husband; their warm friendly faces were brown and as wrinkled as shriveled apples.

"I remember," the farmer began. Nick's heart pounded with excitement; he knew that with those words, a story was forthcoming.

"We were hiding Jews in the caves on our farm and were concerned with that. We had never seen Americans before, but one day there was a dogfight here, nearby." He waved his arm toward the west. "And the American plane was shot down, but the pilot and his copilot jumped out in their parachutes. We could see the big mushrooms floating through the sky. Two men from town got to them before the Fascists did, and they stayed here for a while. Real Americans."

He paused. Nick knew he was thinking about June

of 1944, when one of those American plane's techni-
cal apparatus went haywire and the bomb meant to
destroy the German headquarters in Scansansiano
plummeted like a hawk toward the edge of the piazza
and killed ninety-one people. The Scansansianese knew
it had been a mistake, but the dead were still dead, and
Nick realized that this gracious man was of an age to
have known many of them. As the man spoke, the dev-
astation of that loss of life showed in his crumpled
face.

Eyes shiny with emotion, the old man continued
without mentioning the American bombing, his words
replete with dignity and understanding. "I've been to the
American cemetery outside of Florence, and the small
one at Assisi. Vast fields of crosses and a few Stars of
David, and all of them died trying to help us. I won't
forget it. Most of them were boys, eighteen or nineteen
years old. Like every war."

The wife laid her hand gently on her husband's forearm. "Enough, Lonzo. It's the Befania." Short and stocky,
with strong hands and a generous, warm demeanor, she
turned to Nick and raised her arms for the dance. "You
have to participate to understand."

Nick laughed. "Of course." He slipped the camera
from around his neck, laid it carefully on the edge of
the table, and guided her gently, lovingly into the dance.

The song was a peppy one: "Mamma, Mamma, I saw
the Befana." Towering over the older woman by more
than a foot, Nick jigged around the room, jostling and

bumping along with the other couples as they all stepped lively through the song. Nick noticed that Silvio had taken up the camera from the edge of the table and was helping out by taking photos while Nick danced. On the heels of the closing notes, the musicians sounded the first strains of another song, "Oh Marina," and the farm wife squeezed Nick's hand and moved away to pull another of her guests into the dance.

Flushed and excited, Nick returned to Silvio, who held the camera toward him, and Nick took up where he had left off, and begin snapping photos once again. He had not danced in over ten years, not even with Leah, and had forgotten how much fun it was. In the flush of his dance with the signora, he felt regret that he had not yielded to Leah the few times she had asked him to take her to a dance. Unless compelled by his fieldwork, as on this night, he had difficulty overcoming his natural reticence, in contrast to Leah's impetuous and eager spirit, and now he rued that shyness in himself. You have to participate in order to understand, the signora had told him.

When a half-hour had passed, the musicians struck the first notes of "Maremma Amara," a sad song, followed immediately by "Scansansiano," a love song for the town and countryside. The young women in Nick's group had danced vivaciously to the lively tune of the first songs, but on "Maremma Amara" and "Scansansiano," they stood still, quietly mindful of the melodies, listening with rapt attention. Their eyes reflected those of the family members: A sad yearning and, Nick observed, a love shared by everyone in the room.

The songs over, the Befano and the Befana straightened their clothing: Silvio, dressed as the husband, adjusted his hat and Giovanna, dressed as the wife, centered the wig on her head and retied the scarf, hoping to keep her hairpiece in place for the rest of the evening. Leading the way, the couple moved to the doorway, followed by the rest of the group. The host and his wife followed and stood on the small stone porch waving good-bye. Walking to the cars, one of the young women in the group draped her arm over Andrea's shoulder and Nick heard her say, "Don't let Italo get to you. He shoots his mouth off, but he doesn't really mean it."

The generous emotion Nick had felt dancing in the room was what he loved about his fieldwork, a sense of home at the visceral level. The dancing, food, and yearning among members of a stable community were something he had never experienced.

His own family life, as he was growing up, had been lived in the chaos of his father's angry yelling and his mother's dark, stony silence, which hurt as much as his father's blasts of condemnation. The family turned inward. When friends asked to come over to play, the children begged off. Afraid her husband would erupt in violence, Nick's mother repeatedly cancelled invitations to her friends. The basement family room was dark and silent when it should have been filled with the shouts of raucous play. Then, just when Nick turned ten, his father left them, shattering the family irrevocably. In swift retribution, his mother stormed into court and divorced the man who had been her husband for twenty-five gloomy years. After, she tossed a few household goods into a secondhand trailer and stashed Nick and his two sisters into the back seat. By Nick's senior year in high school, they had moved eight times, each apartment more battered, each of his mother's jobs more menial.

Now, if only as an observer, and even with the warmth and love he had with Leah and Sara, he remembered his childhood and understood that this sense of community was what he had longed for then.

The sensation did not last. In the car with Italo once again, Nick remembered a local proverb: "Who brags, stains himself." He set his teeth for the ride to the next farmhouse, letting his mind wander back to the wizened and gentle hostess at the farm they were rapidly leaving in the distance behind them.

From the woman, Nick's thoughts rushed on to the Antoninis, to Leah and to Giulio's death. Staring into the darkness and the thick web of trees passing in a blur along the roadside, it sobered him to realize anew that this strong sense of community—and murder—could exist side by side.

Chapter Twelve

Entering through the kitchen archway, Anna raised her arm to touch her friend's shoulder. Leah swung around with a shout.

"Leah, it's okay! It's just me." In an impulse of protection, Anna hugged her. "I just wanted to tell you that they're coming. Francesca heard them driving in."

Leah's face flushed a bright red. "I'm sorry. I was concentrating on taking photos of the food, and I guess I had just blanked out everything else."

Anna looked puzzled. "You're nervous tonight. Is everything okay?"

"Yes, it's just . . . well, I guess I've got a lot on my mind. The deadline for the article is coming up, and I haven't yet gotten all the photos I wanted."

"Would you like me to go to the vie cave with you?"

Leah's voice quivered. Susceptible to Anna's kindness, she strained to keep from crying.

"No. It's okay. It's just . . . this murder too."

"Please don't say murder. We don't know for sure yet."

"But . . ." Leah looked into her friend's eyes and Anna read the fear.

"What is it, Leah? There *is* something."

"I can't talk about it. Please don't ask me. I can't say anything yet."

Anna hugged her once again and pulled back, holding Leah at arm's length, a puzzled expression on her face. She considered whether to press Leah or not, but decided against it. "Don't worry. You're safe with us. You don't have to say anything until you want to, or ever, if you don't want. But try not to think about murder. We can't know yet, can we?"

Again Leah flushed, and she turned away. "No. Of course, you're right." She had seen that Anna knew she knew something about Giulio's death, and she sighed, relieved by the patience and trust of her friend.

Arms linked, they passed into the living room just as the cars were pulling up in the broad gravelled space behind the house. Francesca was standing in the open doorway, smiling, waving to the members of the Befania troupe. Leah held back at the far end of the room listening to the singing, wondering which group it would be, suprised when she saw Andrea, and then Nick, come through the doorway.

Darting through the group, she angled her way toward

Nick and put her arms around his neck, fatigued from the intense concentration it took to function for hours in Italian and relieved to whisper in English, "Have you heard anything?"

He looked into her eyes. Her face was drawn and pale. "A little, but I'll have to tell you later. What about you? It must be hard not to say anything. Did Leonardo tell you the story?"

"It's very hard, Nick. Anna has guessed that I know something. But she's so good, so patient, she won't insist."

"Just a little longer. I'm afraid that the general feelings tonight are pretty gloomy—edgy in fact."

"I don't know. I can't promise. It might be better to tell them."

Before Nick could respond, the crowd gathered in a circle. Silvio and Giovanna, Befano and Befana, danced together and drew Leonardo and Anna into the second dance, swinging in lively steps to the music. The others pressed close to the table, which was laden with pizzas, sandwiches, and desserts, and Nick moved about the room snapping photos from different angles to capture the sense of motion and the faces of the Befano and the Befana.

Within minutes everyone was dancing. Italo shouldered his way through the others and held his open palms toward Leah. She took his hands, and they moved forward into the dancers.

"I've had a fine time riding with your husband."

"Oh? And you're . . ."

"Italo."

"Well, Nick is a good companion."

"Yes . . . maybe, what should I say? A little reserved—but *you* don't seem the reserved type. I saw you run to him when he came in." He grinned lasciviously and pulled her close to him.

Leah stiffened and glanced at the other dancers. "Well, he's my husband . . ."

"Yeah, but something new is always exciting, isn't it? Come on. Relax. Let yourself go. It's the Befania."

Repulsed by his smarmy tone, Leah pulled away, noticing as she did that a woman in the Befania group was staring at her and Italo. Leah could imagine the gossip.

"I don't feel well, Italo. I need to stop." She turned and walked away without waiting for his response.

Anna came to stand by Leah.

"The music's lively, Anna, but there's a rim of sadness to it all, isn't there?"

Anna considered what Leah had said. "Perhaps the Befania should have been cancelled this year; I think we're all feeling guilty to be dancing on the day poor Giulio died."

"Or, maybe Giulio would have liked it for you all to be together, remembering him. Like a wake. Think of how we've been talking about him—Leonardo sharing stories of their times at school—and I imagine the others in the cars have been doing the same thing. And think of all the groups coming that didn't know Giulio or know about his death."

The wine the members of the troupe had drunk in the previous two houses began to have its effect and now, drinking again, the members of the Befania group moved into the center of the room to dance. As Leah extended her hand to a little round woman in a bulky sweater and brown housedress who was coming to greet her, Leah could see Italo leering at her.

"Are you friends with the Antoninis?" the woman asked Leah in a feathery voice, taking Leah's hand with both of her own.

Happy, Leah thought, and responded with warmth. "Yes, we've known each other for a while now."

"I think I remember. You were here last year with your husband, no?"

"Yes, I was."

"Taking pictures and recording the music, just like this year." The woman's eyes glistened in the light from the ceiling chandelier.

"That was us." Leah couldn't help smiling.

"I come every year, too. And I like particularly to come here, not only because I've known Leonardo and Anna since we were children, but because Anna makes the best ricciolmo in the whole countryside." She turned and pointed with her finger at the cake behind her on the sideboard. "Have you tried it?"

"Not yet."

"Don't wait or it may be gone!" She tossed her head back and laughed, then moved away, waving at another rotund little woman across the room.

Giovanna, her Befana costume askance, called for a snake dance, and Leah, with everyone else, stepped forward to join in, placing her hands on the shoulders of the one in front of her, winding back and forth in circles and figure eights with the group as the music played. Andrea picked up the tempo. The thread of dancers kept his pace and moved faster and faster about the room, heads bobbling from side to side, their laughter rebounding from the white walls.

When Andrea began another song, Leah stepped away from the twisting line to take a breather, and found Rosetta by the dessert board at the back of the room. Leaning close to be heard over the din, Leah remarked, "That's a beautiful cowboy hat Silvio is wearing."

"Yes, a fine example. Many of the men have them, but just the cheaper ones—for work, you know." Leah could barely hear the words and leaned closer. "They're like your American cowboy hats."

The musicians played at a frenetic, driven pace, as if the community wanted to force the sadness and horror from its midst and let tradition bridge the chasm Giulio's death had created among them. Veering into a curve as the line skirted the dessert buffet, something flew out of Silvio's pocket and bounced off the wall into the middle of the floor. Stefania, one of the young women of the troupe who worked as a clerk in the grocery store near the middle school, stooped to pick it up, and then yelled above the music.

"Hey! This is Giulio's bullet necklace, the one he made in the Army."

At the mention of Giulio's name, Andrea abruptly stopped playing and an ominous silence blanketed the room. Silvio had grabbed at the necklace and was grappling with Stefania to get it away from her. The others in the room watched the two of them, shocked by the impropriety of it.

"Give it to me. It's mine." Silvio's words were warped by his mask, which had slipped and twisted to the side of his face, giving him the appearance of an actual devil.

Stefania stumbled backward, clutching the necklace in her fist, her face a bright red.

"It is *not* yours. It's Giulio's and you know it. You served with him. He told me he was going to give it to someone, a woman he said, as a present."

Silvio pulled off his mask and swung round to Giovanna. His breath was coming in short, sharp spurts, and he spoke in a ragged, rasping voice. "Tell them!"

His broadbrimmed hat cast a shadow over his face, but Leah could see beads of sweat slide down his cheeks and drop off the smooth line of his jaw.

Giovanna flushed with exertion and anger.

In the middle of the Antoninis' living room, riding the memory, she barked at Silvio. "I'll tell them when hell freezes over! That's Giulio's bullet, and I'm wondering how *you* got it? He told me he'd never take it off, some-body'd have to kill him to do it. So just help yourself!" She circled the air with her arm. "Come on everybody, let's get to the next house."

Shocked to silence at the affront to the Antoninis, the group filed out behind Giovanna, with Silvio trailing at the end, his head hanging.

Nick rushed to give Leah a quick kiss. "I'm going to stay with them," he whispered to her, and headed out with the others.

The group gone, Anna, Carla, Francesca, and Leah quietly straightened the trays on the table and began re-plenishing the buffet, carrying in plates mounded high with pizzas. They could hear Tito, still barking as the red taillights of the cars bumped down the rough road toward the highway.

Side by side with Carla, Leah set a heaping plate of sandwiches at the end of the table and dusted the crumbs from the tablecloth into her hand. When Carla turned back toward the kitchen, Leah stopped her with a gentle touch.

"What was that scene between Giovanna and Silvio all about?"

"We say: Love and jealousy are born together. Giulio and Giovanna used to be lovers, or at least close, close friends." Carla shook her head as she spoke.

"But he's so much older . . ."

Carla laughed. "Haven't you seen many older men

stroking their egos with younger women? Remember, Silvio is much older as well." She turned serious. "We all know there are drugs between the three of them, so it's not a lovers' intrigue alone. I don't know all the details, but Silvio and Giulio were in the Army together and they've been good friends, but a triangle is never good. People do evil things." She glanced over her shoulder as if someone might hear.

Chapter Thirteen

Leah and Nick both sat bolt upright when the telephone squealed the next morning at 9 A.M., just four hours after they had gone to sleep. Scrambling for the phone, Leah knocked her book and glasses off the bedstand, and they smacked to the floor.

"Damn it!" she shouted, her voice gravelly from sleep.

"Mom! It's me, Sara. Why are you cursing, and what's with your voice?"

Leah cleared her throat and ignored the remark about the cursing. "Not much sleep."

"I thought Dad would be up inputting his notes already."

"We were tired. Yesterday was exhausting."

"Day? I thought the Befania wasn't until last night, and you're usually back at two or so, aren't you?"

Leah stumbled. "Ah . . . you know, preparation . . ."

"Are you guys fighting again?"

"No. No. Just the opposite in fact."

"Well, that's good because I've got news for you!" Leah could her the child in her voice. "We're coming to see you!"

"Have you already bought the tickets?"

"Well, gee, don't get too excited."

"I'm sorry, I—"

"We're in Prague right now, Mom! Cheap tickets if we came through here, but we had to grab them. Since we postponed the wedding, we could afford it, so we're spending a little time here and then catching Czech Airlines to Rome. I wanted to suprise you, but Jonathan said I'd better not, just in case. And it sounds like it was good I didn't."

Leah had put the wedding out of mind and had not called the florist shop or the people at the hall, or friends helping with the invitations. It would explain her lack of enthusiasm, and she used it.

"It's not that I'm not excited; it's just that I was thinking about how I hadn't done anything. I hadn't even called Genna. When will you come, sweetie?"

"*I* called her, and she's been great. I'm not a baby. Things are under control, and I don't know yet when we'll come." She giggled.

"Why are you giggling?"

"Nothing. Just happy to be talking to you."

"You never giggled before when you talked to me."

Sara giggled again.

"Okay. Giggle away. I won't ask."

"Good. Anyway, we want to poke around Prague for a little—but you still don't sound very excited about us coming." Her voice had an edge of blame.

"I'm just tired. We got in very, very late—or early, I should say."

"Okay. Listen, I've got to go. Johnny's waiting for me in the lobby. We'll see you soon. Love ya."

"Me too. Be safe."

Leah turned to Nick. "They're in Prague and they're coming here."

"Oh no! When?" He leaned up on his elbow, rubbing his face.

"She wouldn't say. They want to see Prague, but I don't think it will be long."

"Oh God. Let's just hope it's after all this is settled."

The narrow streets of Scansansiano reminded Leah of the vie cave. On both sides, houses of tufa stone rose high above her and Nick, blocking the sunshine. Shored by strong shots of coffee after Sara's call, they were walking up the hill toward the police station.

"I hope they aren't coming soon." In a habitual gesture, Nick ran his fingers through his hair.

When he dropped his arm, Leah took his hand and held it as they walked, to keep him from pulling out any

more hair. "We'll get through it. It's just going to be difficult to concentrate. I think we'll have to explain, because they'll hear about it one way or the other."

"Okay. We'll be positive. Prague is beautiful. Maybe
they won't be here for several days. So, for now, we'll
just deal with the police and won't worry about them."
He was talking to himself again, in his lecture mode.

Unnoticed by Nick, Leah turned and smiled at him,
but said nothing.

The police station was on the far side of the piazza
in one of the ancient dwellings that centuries before had
belonged to the nobility. Leah and Nick entered through
a long walkway guarded by two stone lions. The pathway
ended in steep steps to a wide oak doorway with a giant
iron ring handle. Nick pulled on the handle and the door
opened into a foyer, bare except for an umbrella stand.
They passed through double glass doors into the outer
office.

Signorina MacCleod sat at the reception desk, her
long red hair frizzed and wild about her face. She looked
up as they came in.

"Ah. It's you. Visas, no? Or"—she smiled wickedly,
continuing in a deep bass—"have you come to confess
to murder?"

Nick and Leah spoke at the same time, their faces
suddenly flushed. "Visas."

Signorina MacCleod laughed. "Of course visas. So
why turn so red?" Still laughing, she stood, showing a

long expanse of bare leg below a short black wool skirt that ended ten inches above high-heeled black boots. "I'll tell the lieutenant. He's only here for a few minutes, so you're lucky to catch him. He is *very* busy with all this murder or suicide or accident business—or whatever it was." Swinging her hips in sinuous motion for Nick's benefit, she crossed the floor and knocked on Lieutenant Cavour's door.

A tall lean man, in his mid-forties, with thick dark hair, chestnut eyes, and a mustache, Cavour was an imposing figure and was not happy to see them. "I'm sorry, Signorina MacCleod should not have shown you in. I don't have time to spare."

Nick glanced over his shoulder. MacCleod had left the door ajar. He turned back and gently pulled it closed, while Leah watched. Cavour's eyebrows raised in curiosity. Nick approached the desk and leaned over to speak in a low voice.

"It's about the murder that we've come."

Cavour raised his head with such force that he felt one of his neck muscles seize. It was a stabbing pain, but accustomed to controlling himself and too dignified not to, he raised his hand to massage his neck as if in thought. After a short pause, he responded, matching Nick's low voice, the only sign of his surprise and pain manifesting in a hiss: "Murder? We have no proof of that."

Leah stepped forward and spoke in an even lower voice. "I know it was murder. I saw it."

For an instant, Cavour's reserve faltered. "Santa

Madonna!" He cleared his throat, straightened his uniform jacket, and sat down, motioning to two chairs in front of his desk. "Sit." It was a command and Leah and Nick, like obedient dogs at the voice of a master, sat in unison.

"Speak." The lieutenant was composed once again.

Leah described for him in one long breath how she had walked up the via cava to take pictures and found the spot where she could get a good shot of the table rock. She rushed on to tell how, taking the photo, the camera had delayed because she had bungled the timer, and in that delay she had seen—and photographed inadvertently—one man pushing another man off the cliff and then the killer had seen her and chased her to one of the necropoli where she had hidden, and then he had found her out and had come into the cave, poking in the crevices, and then Nick had whistled and the killer had escaped.

When she finished, she drew in a long breath.

Angered at this new development, which would change the investigation, the lieutenant's voice was barely controlled. "And why didn't you come yesterday?"

"We did. But you were both out, and the note read that you would not be in. We were afraid to tell anyone, or to say anything over the phone."

He grunted and shook his head. "Do you have the camera with you?"

Leah gave it to him. "And I brought the cord, so you could upload it to your computer. The photo is the last but one. Just click 'mode.'"

"I'm familiar with digital cameras, Signora." He took the camera, and pressed the button at the top to turn it on. A photo blossomed on the tiny monitor. He clicked once on the left side of the dial to find the previous picture, and the murder appeared.

The lieutenant squinted at the tiny screen. "It's too small here to see. Of course. I'll bring it up on computer and enlarge the figures."

"Yes, but . . ." Leah glanced at Nick. Nick took her hand and spoke for her.

"We need to make sure that Leah is safe. Everyone, including your secretary, thinks we are here because of our visas, and we would appreciate it if no one knows the real reason we're here."

"Do I seem an amateur to you, Signor Contarini?"

Nick blushed. "No. Of course not. It's just that we—"

"I know how to protect my witnesses, Signor, but—" Seeing their fear, he stopped himself. For an instant, his generous and gentle nature, generally hidden under cover of his uniform, broke through the tough exterior he had constructed for his work. "No one else, and particularly Signorina MacCleod."—he indicated the door by a slight tilt of his chin—"will know of it. But let me suggest one thing: Stick to your research on the Befania. Perhaps read a few more books in the comfort and safety of your apartment. I'll have my man pass by a few times on his walks around town, to check on you."

Nick eyes opened wide. "How did you know about my research on the Befania?"

"Madonna!" Cavour brought his palms together, shaking them up and down. "Everyone that rents to foreigners fills out paperwork for our office—you yourself filled out the paperwork."

"But I only said 'research.' "

"This is a small town, signor. I know more about you, and many others, than you can imagine. It's my business. But you needn't worry. I'm perfectly discreet, and I think it is a fine thing to research our Befania. It's unique."

He paused and flashed a brilliant white smile. "And really, how can you wonder about yourselves? Two Americans, to use your expression, 'stick out like a sore thumb.' "

He laughed and rose from his chair, indicating the door. "Now, please . . . I'll be in touch with you."

"But can't we bring up the photo now? I want to know who tried to kill me."

Cavour straightened his shoulders and his smile turned to a frown. "It is in my hands now, Signora; I will take care of everything. This is police business, not for civilians, and certainly not for foreigners. Go home, back to your research, and you, Signora"—he wiggled his finger at Leah—"no more walks on the vie cave for now, even if you do need photos. Your magazine can wait, I think."

Leah stared hard at him. He was right: The magazine *could* wait, but she would walk where she wanted.

Chapter Fourteen

They crossed the piazza toward home. Leah glanced back at the station. "I know we've got to get ready for the cenone tonight, but tomorrow I'm going to go back up to the table rock and see what I can find. There must be something, some small clue they missed."

"Leah! You almost got killed, damn it! Didn't you hear what the lieutenant said?" Nick wanted to enjoy the Befania's group celebratory supper that evening without worrying about Leah running off again.

She took his arm and shook it gently to quiet him. "You don't need to yell so the whole town hears." A covey of men standing in front of the bar were staring at them.

He jerked his arm away. "I do need to yell—you're so stubborn. And the cenone *is* important, so don't even

122

think about going back up there. We're going to go home and study. And read. And we're going to listen to what the lieutenant said, and I don't want you to interfere any more."

She had learned not to argue with Nick, but her own stubbornness tinted her words. "Okay. Okay. Just read and study, and think about the cenone."

They turned into the bar for a cappucino and a brioche before taking the lower street home. Leah was quiet, distracted; she was imagining herself the next morning, on the table rock, finding what the police had missed. The thought pleased her.

At the station, Cavour buzzed Signorina MacCleod. "Get Montaro on the phone and tell him I need to see him as soon as possible."

"What shall I tell him it's about."

"You don't need to tell him it's about anything, Signorina. Just tell him to get over here now!"

Cavour had no idea how to bring up the photo on his computer. He hoped Montaro did.

Chapter Fifteen

That night, the members of the Befania group met in the piazza. Nick and Leah stood shoulder to shoulder, shivering in the damp cold, listening to the others chatter in excited anticipation of the cenone, the big meal the group would make from the food they had collected, following the tradition. Silvio and Giovanna were holding hands as if nothing had happened between them the night before, and Angelina stuck to Italo's side like a cocklebur, cooing into his neck, snickering. While they all waited for Stefania and her friend, they stood near the bar chatting—those who smoked twirled their cigarettes to shake off the ashes before they brought them again to their mouths.

When Stefania arrived, accompanied by her friend, Primo, they walked in ragged lines of twos and threes down the narrow, darkened streets, where cats hunkered on the top steps of raised doorways and the bedclothes and pillowcases of preoccupied housewives flapped in the damp night air above them. Near the butcher shop, they turned down a small side street and from that into another narrow way, darker than the one before. A few houses down, Andrea stopped in front of a wooden door, and the others gathered behind him as he dug a key from his pocket and pulled a flashlight out of the bag he was carrying. Nick put his arm around Leah's shoulder, pulling her close to him. "Exciting huh?" She nodded, watching Andrea place the key.

Once he had opened the door, the others filed through, down a wide stone stairwell to Giulio's aunt's cantina. Straight through the room was a doorway leading out to a long terrace that spanned the length of the cantina and hung over the gorge, which sliced through the forests below the town. On the terrace, to the side, were two fruit trees and a patch of flowers, just outside the doorway of a smaller adjoining apartment, where Signora Seta, Giulio's aunt, kept some kitchen things and a few chairs. To the sharp right at the bottom of the stairwell was a ramp descending into the cantina itself, where barrels of wine hunkered on hewn stone platforms. The temperature was a perfect 11 degrees Centigrade. The cave-like room, with a rounded stone ceiling, had centuries before been dug out of the tufa below a three-story house. Straight on was a large, high-ceilinged room, curved at the top. The graceful sweeping motions of the workmen who had hewn the stone were evident in the half-curve cut marks, as if they had been painted there from an artist's brush, rising and falling, one after the other, like waves of water.

"Have you seen Signora Seta then?" Italo asked Andrea.

"No. Nobody's seen her."

Nick interjected. "I heard someone say she went down somewhere on the coast to meet a friend of hers from Rome, but nobody knows where they're staying."

Italo snorted. "Sounds like she had everything planned in advance. Maybe she's the one who did away with Giulio."

"Don't be stupid." Andrea glared at Italo. "They've called all over to try to find out. She'll turn up, and the news will be a great shock to her. Now let's do this." He dangled the key in the air.

Giovanna had overheard Italo. "You idiot. Don't talk that way—and stop intimating that it's murder. Giulio fell. He tripped or something, and that's all there is to it, and now he's gone." Her voice quivered and tears pooled in her eyes.

Italo leered at her. "And now he's gone. And so, boo-hoo, is your drug source."

"Fool! You're not even from here, even if you do come here all the time because we're so tra-di-tion-al and you just love that; you're just a salesman who wants to pretend that he's from here, wants to pretend he's some sort of Tiburzi while he sells the newest Fiats to people who can't afford them."

Angelina, who was hovering next to Italo like a rabbit, turned a bright red and in one swift motion raised her hand as if to strike Giovanna. Silvio caught her wrist midair.

"Okay. Okay. Giovanna, back off and Angelina—"

"What?" She spit the word, staring intently at Silvio, trying to twist her arm free.

He held her tightly. "Calm yourself. Nobody's going to hurt Italo. Giovanna didn't mean it. We're just all on edge because of Giulio's death. Come on. Let's just have the cenone and try to remember that Giulio would have loved this. He would have wanted us to be singing and remembering him with good stories and wine. Okay?"

Angelina nodded and Silvio dropped her wrist.

When the others had moved through the doorway, Silvio turned to Giovanna with a smile on his lips. "My God, what's with *her* tonight?"

Giovanna sniggered. "She's his girlfriend, but I'd be afraid to get in bed with her." Giggling, intimate once more, they followed the others into the building.

When they first entered the stairwell from the street, Leah had failed to notice a door immediately to the right at the top of the stairs. Now, they all trooped up the stairs and stepped through this doorway. Another short flight of steps led to a wide, low–ceilinged room with a stove in one corner and a table next to it. A line of chairs sat along the opposite wall. Each one took a chair and then started down the broad stairway again, to the cantina. As they descended, the air took on a still chill she hadn't felt coming off the street, and, for a moment, Leah was reminded of the burial cave where she had hidden from the killer. She shuddered, took a deep breath, remembered where she was, and that she was surrounded by friends.

Traipsing awkwardly downward, each wrestling with a chair in front of them, they came to the lower landing, where they shuffled to the right, wrangling the straight-backed chairs through a broad archway that led into the wider room. Leah noticed there were enigmatic openings to narrow passageways no larger than the spine of a fairly large book, situated high up in the walls.

She set her chair on the rough tufa floor, passed back through the archway and started toward the steps to fetch another chair, but decided instead to take a closer look at the darkened cavern down the ramp.

"That's the cantina itself." Primo, a tall, thin man who had been in the Befania group, saw her peering into the darkness. "I've got a flashlight, would you like to go in?"

"Very much, thanks."

With careful steps, they descended the gentle slope of the ramp. Primo's flashlight was small, with a dull light that spread a glow only a few feet. As they passed into the darkness, the weak light faintly illuminated giant barrels of wine arranged in lines along both walls.

"A perfect 11 degrees." Primo explained what Leah already knew, but she listened carefully, tilting her head to his darkened form. He spoke with gentle authority. "The constant temperature means that these cantinas, here on the north side of town, are very valuable to people who make and sell wine, or even if they just want to make wine for themselves. It's rare they are for sale. A wine dealer would kill to have one of these."

"Kill?"

"Sorry. An unfortunate slip. I'm really sorry. It's an expression. It's just that a cantina like this is valuable and Signora Seta is lucky to have it. But it's beautiful as well in its way, isn't it? Look at the walls, so perfect, so evenly chipped."

"I was noticing earlier. The grace of the workmen shows."

"You have a good eye." He smiled, gratified that she understood the aesthetic. "Do you have good taste as well? Which one of our wines do you like best?"

Leah laughed at the sudden switch in subject. The locals were always asking her which wines she liked best, and if the local wines were better than those of Piedmonte or the Veneto.

"Don't try to trick me. I'm a visitor here and I don't want to make enemies by naming the wrong wine."

He laughed. "Ah, you're quick . . . and politic."

"Really, it is very difficult for me to say which one is best. I like them all!"

"Do you mean all Italian wines, or all of the Scansansiano wines?"

She touched his arm, laughing, "Only the local, Primo. I only drink local wine."

He joined in her laughter and nodded. "You are resolutely diplomatic. But we *do* have the best wines. It's true. And it is difficult to choose among them sometimes."

"Yes, so I'm doing my best to try them all."

In the dim light, she missed his warm smile.

"On another matter." They were moving toward the outer room as Primo spoke. "Nick mentioned to me that Italo has been telling him about the vie cave and Tiburzi. You shouldn't listen to everything Italo says. He's not an expert, and he likes to make things a bit more dramatic than they actually are. The vie cave were not mysterious deep pathways carved out by the Etruscans."

Leah thought of her article. "They weren't?"

"No. The pathways were there and the Etruscans used them, but I don't believe the theory that they orginally carved them that deep. I think it was through centuries of use that they became so deep."

"Yes, I've read that theory, but what about the burial caves along the sides?"

They walked back up the ramp. Just as Primo started to explain his own theory, which she knew was disputed, Leah was distracted by a hole about the size of a bushel basket at the top of the ramp, to the side.

"What's that for?"

"Take a look."

She bent and peered into the hole. It opened, she saw, on a huge, round cavern dug deep below.

Primo bent beside her. "Some people say it was for burials, but I think it was just for refuse. Not food or perishable things, but bits of stone, pieces of wood and such. A place for the dirt and stone they dug out to make the cantina—and probably not as old as the Etruscans."

"It smells bad. Rotten, like a carrion flower."

"What's that?"

"It's a flower that smells like a dead animal, to attract flies and beetles. It's even flesh-colored and has hair."

"Ich! Let me get a little closer."

Leah moved to the side, and Primo leaned his head into the opening. "My light's not too bright, but it doesn't look like there's much in this one but some stone chips. It might be from another apartment or room. Did you see those narrow airways high up on the wall in the other room?"

"Yes, what are they?"

"They're found in some of these refuse holes as well, and they often connect with each other, so maybe someone left something to rot in one of the other dump holes or in an adjoining cantina or apartment. I don't know." He brushed his hand through the air. "Let's get the rest of the chairs."

Chapter Sixteen

Manoeuvering the turns, Silvio and Andrea finessed a long folding table down the steps and set it up in the middle of the room. Stefania shuffled the chairs into place around it.

"Sit, everybody. The omelettes and sausages are almost ready." She ran back through the archway and up the stairs to the makeshift kitchen. While Primo opened the bottles of wine they had been given the night before and poured for everyone, Andrea hefted his accordion onto his lap, slipped his arms through the straps and sounded the first notes of one of the Befania songs.

"May I?" Leah indicated a seat beside Italo and Angelina.

Still sitting, Italo pulled the chair out for her. She smiled at him, but noticed that Angelina was scowling, and decided differently. "Thanks, Italo, but I think I'll move around beside Angelina. I can be closer to the music then, and I like it loud, almost earsplitting."

Leah had learned from interviewing men that she could be a source of tension to other women. A foreigner was possessed of a certain exoticism; as an unknown she knew she could be suspect, so she had learned to make sure to speak openly with all the people around her to demonstrate that she was committed in her marriage, friendly but not overly so, and professional.

Italo motioned Primo to move over a chair on the other side of Angelina, who was now facing forward with an icy stare. She made no acknowledgment when Leah sat beside her. Leah persisted.

"What sort of work do you do, Angelina?"

Angelina grunted and leaned toward Leah in a mean whisper: "Do you think moving beside me hides the fact that you're after Italo?"

"What?" Leah looked her straight in the face.

"I saw the way you looked at him." Angelina's face had contorted in angry jealousy. "And you'll learn not to do it. He's mine!" She faced Leah full on and tapped her chest with her index finger.

"Come on, Angelina, I don't even know Italo!"

"That's not what I've heard."

"What?"

"I heard you were dancing close with him at the Befania."

Leah remembered her short exchange with Italo at the

Neta Seffer

Antoninis' house. In any other situation she would have laughed, but Angelina's voice was so thick with hatred it made Leah angry. "Well, you got it wrong." This time she was the one to spit out the words.

"I don't think so. And don't try to pretend you've never seen me before." Angelina leaned even more closely toward her, as if in challenge.

"That's weird. I don't know if I have or not; maybe from a distance . . ."

"Oh, when was that?"

"I don't know." Exasperated, Leah's voice had a hard, commanding edge. "Look. Let's start over. I have no interest in Italo. Why not talk about work?"

Angelina straightened and Leah, too, sat upright.

"Why? Are you thinking of writing an article on my very interesting life?"

"No, just conversation."

"For conversation's sake then." Her voice was pure sarcasm. "I'm a real estate agent. Not exactly as exotic as being a writer who can afford to travel all the time, is it?"

"I didn't mean any offense."

"I'm sure." She spoke through clenched teeth. Her breath was bad.

Leah took a deep breath. "Look, there's no reason to be sarcastic; if you don't want to talk, we don't have to, or we could choose some neutral subject. There's no reason to create bad feelings on a night like tonight."

Angelina refused to let go. "A neutral subject? Like Giulio's death, maybe?" Eyes wide, she stared at Leah.

"I wouldn't call it neutral, but at least it's not about us."

"No, it isn't, and I don't care a fig what happened to him."

"But it was horrible."

"Lots of life is horrible. Why should I care? I only met him once or twice."

Leah was dumbfounded by Angelina's callous attitude and the way she rushed on, compelled it seemed, to explain. Her voice had changed and she spoke as if Leah weren't there. "My God! I didn't think about him. It was business with him and his aunt—arrangements . . . about this place actually."

"Oh?"

"But it fell through, so I didn't pay any more attention." She shifted uncomfortably in her seat and stared at Leah, as if to challenge her.

"You seem so cold about it, and yet you are obviously a tender woman." Leah had seen her holding Italo's hand. She took it to be a public expression of affection of a sort she rarely saw in Italy, except among teenagers.

Angelina followed Leah's gaze and looked down at her own hand, clasped around Italo's.

"Maybe I'm not tender at all; maybe I just don't want Italo to get—or be taken—away. And I'd like to listen to the music if you don't mind?"

Leah expelled a breath through her lips and scooted her chair a few inches backward.

One by one, as Andrea played, they all joined in, singing the songs they had sung the night before at the Befania. Italo stood, took Angelina's hand and led her away from the table so they could dance. A bit taller than Italo, her movements, contrary to Italo's grace, were stiff; like wooden sticks she shifted them from step to step and held the top part of her body rigid, thick as a stone column, though cloyingly close to Italo.

After the dance, Andrea, under the influence of a quick four glasses of wine, called for Leah and Nick to sing an American song.

"An Am–er–i–can song! Put your cam–er–a a–way and sing Am–er–i–can songs!" He pounded the table with both fists as he chanted in heavy rhythm, and the others soon joined in.

Nick whispered to Leah, "Okay. How about one of the Child Ballads?"

"No, Nick!" she hissed. "The only Child Ballads I know are about murders. Actually the only one I really know is 'The Willow Tree.'"

"Oh, yeah." He thought for a minute, anxious to come up with something. The group's shouting made it difficult to concentrate.

"Look, they're not going to know the English, except maybe a few words."

She clenched her teeth, attempting to disguise her

words, though most of the others would not understand what she was saying anyway. "It's still a murder . . ."

"Come on Leah, we have to do this; they've been really generous with us."

"I just wish I knew another song, that wasn't about a push off the cliff."

"It'll be okay. It's a different sort of shove off a cliff." Nick grinned.

"Shhh! They'll hear you!" She grasped his arm, shaking it lightly, as if he could think of another song for her. "Okay, okay, I've got it."

"What is it?"

" 'How Many Miles to Babylon.' "

"That's good. Come on." He turned to Andrea and reverted to Italian. "Okay. Here goes." He faced Leah. "On the count of three: One, two, three . . ."

> *"How many miles to Babylon?*
> *Three score and ten.*
> *Can we get there by candlelight?*
> *There and back again.*
>
> *Open the gate and let us pass.*
> *Gold you must pay.*
> *Gold I have none, what shall I do?*
> *Turn and walk away."*

The song was somber and pale, almost monotone, compared to the natural verve of the Befania songs, and when they finished, the others clapped politely, and nodded in goodwilled sympathy. Without saying anything, Andrea hoisted his accordion onto his lap once more.

"Wait." Giovanna came through the doorway, a large platter in her hands. "Let's eat and then we can sing again."

The platter was piled high with crispy sausages and huge round omelettes. Primo poured another round of wine and they all dug in, cheered by the food, jovially reaching across one another for more.

When the platter was empty, Stefania lugged an enormous shopping bag from near the doorway, put it on the table, and pulled out cakes and biscotti, some from the houses they had visited and some from the bakery.

"Wait!" Andrea spread out his hands to stop everyone from reaching for the sweets. "Signora Seta wanted us to have some of her famous Luisa Seta fragolino wine from two years ago. Remember how sweet and smooth it was? I'd almost forgotten." He waved a long, thick key in the air. "It's in the other little cantina, I'll go get it."

Italo jumped up, upsetting a glass of wine that spilled in a red sea across the table. "Ughh. Sorry. Do you want me to get it, Andrea, while you go ahead and play?"

Angelina slipped her arm through Italo's pulling him back into his chair. "You're not a servant. Let him go." She smirked, tilting her head toward the others. "They should be waiting on you, not you on them."

Andrea settled it. "Thanks. I promised the Signora I

wouldn't give the key to anyone else, so I'd better do it myself." He turned to Primo. "Can I use your flashlight?"

Primo handed him the light, and Andrea stepped under the archway to the terrace door. Outside, he turned to the other, smaller door. The key fit smoothly into the lock; and he walked in.

A foul smell made him jerk and wretch.

"Uhhch!" He pulled his shirt front up over his nose, and moved toward the refrigerator, which he could just make out in the dim light. Near the ramp that led to his left, down into the cantina of the apartment, he tripped on a small stepstool, and the flashlight tumbled out of his hand into the refuse hole.

"Devil take it!" He dropped down on his knees, and crawled carefully toward the hole, faintly illuminated by the light that had fallen to the bottom. At the edge of the hole, he peered in.

"Ahhh!" Andrea turned his head and vomited.

Chapter Seventeen

"Nobody within three meters of the doorway. Back!"

Lieutenant Cavour, a glove clamped over his nose and mouth, was in a foul mood. He did not like being awakened at night, and he did not like it that there was another dead body, and he did not like the smell. It wasn't that he was unaccustomed to bad smells; he had been raised on a small farm a few kilometers outside of town, and his father had cattle, two horses, and a few pigs. But dead human bodies emitted a fetid odor unlike the warm, almost sweet smell of living animal hide and manure, and he had never become accustomed to the odor of corpses, even fresh ones, which this one was not.

The group hovered together in a tight circle outside the doorway where Signora Seta had been found. The others pelted Andrea with questions, but Andrea stood at the edge of the terrace, staring out over the gorge. When Italo put his arm around Andrea's shoulder, Andrea shrugged it off, and Angelina pulled Italo away.

"Let him be. He doesn't want us around right now." She flung a hand out toward the others. "And they don't either."

"But we have to stay. They'll want to ask questions."

"What are you talking about? I know you're upset, but don't be foolish. It's chaos here now, and there's no reason to stay. He said they would question everyone tomorrow in the office."

"Okay, okay." Italo acquiesed easily; he wanted to go, and he was glad to have Angelina take control.

Inside, the lieutenant had tied a rope under the arms of Sergeant Gianicollo, and after helping him tie a handkerchief over his face, lowered the smaller man into the hole, to identify the body. They all knew it was Signora Luisa, but the lieutenant had to make certain. He wished he could bring her up and give her the dignity of being in the funeral home. He had known her all his life and, mixed with the disgust of the odor and the deathly distortion of the corpse's limbs which reflected none of Signora Luisa's lively living warmth, was saddened and angered that he was forced by his duty as a police officer to wait until the scene could be thoroughly inspected, even though he knew the area was already compromised.

At the bottom of the hole, kneeling on a towel he had dropped under his feet, Gianicollo gently pulled the hair aside—then turned away and vomited violently against the curved wall.

"Pull me up!" he shouted. "It's her!" He had barely spoken the words when he gagged again, repeatedly. When a small stream of yellowish liquid was all that oozed from his lips, he wiped his shirt sleeve across his mouth.

They hauled him out of the hole. Once off the rope, he rushed, pale and trembling, to the open doorway for air.

It was a few minutes before he spoke. "Her head is bashed in from the back, and her bowels must have gone because there's . . . stuff all over the place."

Cavour passed Gianicollo, through the doorway and spoke to the others. "It is Signora Luisa Seta. I'll need to take statements from all of you, but not tonight. Give the sergeant your names and addresses and phone numbers, and I'll call you in tomorrow. Be by your phones. I'll want you in one at a time, and I don't want to have to chase you all over the countryside to get in touch."

"Are all the phones working now?"

"Yes, don't worry." The fatigue showed in his voice.

"What about Italo and Angelina?"

"I told them to go. I already talked to Angelina and got their information, and Primo's too. Italo and Angelina are driving back toward Viterbo for the night, and Primo had to get home as well. They're coming in tomorrow."

He paused, looking directly and steadily at each in turn. "Like the rest of you, right?"

Silent, the others nodded.

After Leah and Nick had helped clean up the dinner, they walked home through the darkened streets. Leah held his arm. They leaned into each other, as if for the warmth of contact, and for safety.

"This is creepy, Nick. I'm beginning to wonder if there wasn't something to that little tiff between Andrea and Italo."

"What was it? I feel like my brain's addled, and I don't remember well."

"You know. The first house you went to last night. You told me Italo said that Andrea would be glad if Giulio were dead. If I understood you, it was because Signora Seta would have given Andrea the cantina and those old photos if Giulio decided on moving down south like he'd talked about.

"Yeah. There is something funny there, and it may be true about Andrea, but I just can't accept it. We've known him for a long time."

"And if it was for the photos, they would have to be some photos."

"Yeah, but Andrea is so passionate about his photography that it could have been just for possession and not for money. And anyway, it seems Giulio did have other irons in the fire. I had heard Miss Redhead in the piazza saying that there was some woman in the south who owned a bar, and he was thinking maybe to join her. I guess Giulio and that woman from the south are an item, though it seems like Giulio may have had a few *items* . . ."

Leah wrinkled her nose. "That's one way to put it. And Giovanna was one of them from what the Antoninis said. And who knows? Maybe there were others, if he was the kind to really get around. Think of the Child Ballad we were about to sing. Love can readily turn to jealousy and hate. And with drugs involved . . . But do you think Giovanna could have done it?"

"Physically she's strong enough if somebody's not expecting it. So, maybe, but then why the Signora?" Nick stopped for a minute, and stared off into the darkness as if he might see some answer, and then went on, without speaking. Their footsteps resounded and echoed against the stones of the street and facades of the houses.

"It seems like Giovanna's anger would be toward Giulio," Leah said. "But are you thinking there's some connection between Giovanna and the cantina—or the photos?"

"I don't know. I wonder about Silvio too. He would have to have had a connection as well, either to the cantina or the photos, or both, for the double murders to make sense."

"I guess we're assuming the same person killed Giulio and his aunt, right?"

"It's logical, isn't it? It would be too coincidental otherwise. How many murderers do you think you'd find in a small Tuscan town? Unless, I suppose, two people were working together."

"I didn't think of that." She pulled a tissue from her pocket and blew her nose loudly.

"Geez." Nick laughed. "You'll wake the whole street."

"Sorry. I can't tell if it's the humidity and cold, or if I'm weeping a little. It's all upsetting."

Nick pulled her to him and they walked on. "Who knows who else could be involved? Nobody that we know really seems likely; they just don't. I can't believe we could have misjudged anyone so badly."

"None of this seems likely. But I'm beginning to feel that, except for the Antoninis, we don't really know anyone here, so how do we know what's likely?"

"Let's rethink Italo. He's looking for a restaurant, right. So maybe he wasn't interested in the photos, but he was in the cantina, and Andrea was the reverse: He wanted the photos, but not the cantina."

"In that case, they could have done an amicable exchange, if Andrea inherited. So it would make sense to kill Giulio given the will was in his name, and Andrea was second in line, but it wouldn't make sense to kill the Signora."

"Unless he needed money right away and wanted to get the photos soon. She was in pretty good health from what I hear, and she could have lasted a long time."

"I guess, but like I said, I don't know about the money.

Andrea seems way more interested in the photos themselves."

"You're right. I really think one of these days someone from *National Geographic* will discover him, and he won't need to worry about money anyway. I'm going to buy one of his portraits before we go—if I get out of here alive." She laughed.

Nick stopped short and turned to kiss the top of her head. "I'm going to make sure you *do* get out of here alive, but for me to do that, you have to stay close; you can't go off on your own."

Chapter Eighteen

The next morning at first light, Leah slipped out of bed, carefully lifted her clothes from the back of the chair at the desk, and tiptoed into the living room. She dressed quietly, took her jacket and a house key from off the hooks at the entryway and, turning the handle slowly, edged out, closing the door silently.

Tucking her arms into the sleeves of her jacket, she headed toward the town center. She knew that on the piazza the main bar would be open, and she scuttled through the damp cold air toward it for coffee before she descended into the gorge and then up again on the other side to the via cava. The narrow streets were quiet in the muted light, and Leah relished the chill of the morning air. At Via Vezzosa she glanced to the side toward the little piazza that hung over the gorge and could see the clouds drifting below. It was too beautiful a sight to pass up, and she turned off the main street on the narrow walkway that descended to the piazzetta, where she could have a full view of the gorge.

Leaning over the wall, she spotted a flock of sheep that dotted a meadow by the river, and she could see the roof of what had been the old mill, where, Carla had told her, the women used to go to do their laundry in the river and where the young people went to picnic on Sunday afternoons.

At a slight movement behind her, Leah twirled around. On the bench in the far corner, someone was wrapped head to toe in blankets and appeared to be sleeping. Leah's heart pounded; she moved away from the wall toward the street, but as she did, the man under the blankets poked his head out and, blinking his eyes, looked at her as if to ask *What are you doing here?*

"Good morning, Secondo. I'm sorry I woke you." Her voice carried the tension she felt in her neck and back. Though Nick had said he was harmless, she remembered the strange glee on his face when there was a fight outside the bar, and she eased toward the walkway that led to the street.

His hair was long and oily, a mass of dark tangles that Leah doubted could be brushed straight without repeated washings and much patience. He was a handsome man. His high forehead, acquiline nose, and olive skin were stereotypically Italian and even though spending the night out had left him disheveled, and though he obviously needed a good scrub, Leah realized that at one time, if there had been a time for him, he must have broken hearts.

Secondo stared at her silently. Embarrassed, Leah stopped edging toward the street and stood still. She had called him "Chicken Man" between Nick and herself. Now, facing him, she wondered how she had been so thoughtlessly mean.

She had meant no harm by the nickname; he reminded her of another man, a chicken farmer who lived outside the little town where she had grown up. Originally, the man had a thriving business, but it had dwindled to only ten or twelve chickens, just enough for a few eggs for himself and a few to sell for a pittance to neighbors. That man, too, had lived on the edge of society, keeping to himself, wandering disheveled and dirty around town, in and out of the stores on rainy days. He was friendly enough; he greeted people in a taciturn way, but Leah remembered how all the same people had tapped their heads with their index fingers and smiled when he had gone on his way. It was an act of petty cruelty, and she had been part of it, she now realized. She had been part of it without giving it a thought.

But while on the one hand people had engaged in this sort of ignorant behavior and gossip, on the other hand they were generous in their acts and allowed this physical generosity to excuse the pettiness of their speech. No one bothered Chicken Man, and one of them always left food and clothing on his doorstep.

Ironically, years later, after this shadow of her home-town had died and the sheriff had come to take Chicken Man's body, the officer had found thousands of dollars in the cold mouth of the man's stove, under his mattress, and in the gallon-sized tin cans that he had stored at the back of his foul-smelling cupboards. For years, he had invested his money, living frugally, or worse, and letting his profits literally pile up.

With those memories, Leah faced Secondo. Though she still felt wary and struggled to stay calm, she realized how cold it must have been for him to spend the night on the bench. She reached into her pocket, retrieved the liras she had gotten in change from her groceries a few days before, and handed the money to Secondo, wishing she could have done it in a more gracious way, but not withholding the act because of circumstances.

Reminding herself of something she had read about giving, Leah looked directly in his eyes. "Bless you, Secondo, have some coffee and brioche. It will soon warm up a little bit."

He stared at her, holding her gaze, looked down at the money in his hand, and then back at her. Then, he did something Leah hadn't expected. He set the money down on the pavement and reached his hand toward her. She held out her own, taking his smooth palm, suprised by his gentle but firm grip. His voice was deep and mellow.

"Thank you. I left my money at home and now I won't have to go back to get it before I have coffee. Don't worry about me, Signora. I like sleeping outside, even when it's cold. It's less lonely seeing the stars."

Sabina, the young woman who had the early shift at the bar, broke off her conversation and greeted Leah cheerfully. "You're up bright and early this morning! The usual cappucino?"

"Please."

The old man sitting at one of the tables who had been talking to Sabina grunted in frustration at having his conversation interuppted. He downed his glass of grappa and slammed the empty glass on the table.

Sabina hunched her shoulders, shook her head and turned back to Leah. "What are you up to so early— and without that handsome husband of yours?"

"Oh, just a walk on the via cava."

The old man, Leo, grumbled, his gray head bent over a second glass of grappa that was sitting ready next to the first. Retired, he had been a postal worker, but was ill suited to it. It would have been better if he had been a farmer or a shepherd, some work where he could have been alone most of the time, with visits to the bar in the off hours to chat with the young women who tended the counter. At the post office, he hated greeting the endless string of people with all their picky complaints about bills and packages, who joggled each other for a better place in line. Now that he could come to the bar early every morning and have it to himself except for Sabina, he didn't like it when anyone else came in, though they inevitably did, and he groused and complained, perpetually angry at the invasion of the morning ritual with the young barmaid he had imagined for himself.

"You'd be better off staying away from those trails. Not a very damn pleasant place to walk, I'd say, not these days."

Leah turned to him, suprised by his gruff attitude. "I know. Creepy, but I've got to finish an article I'm working on."

"A what?" He cupped his ear in his hand and leaned forward.

Sabina cut Leo off before he got started on a tirade, as he usually did about tourists and foreigners, and smiled warmly at Leah. "Well, just be safe."

"Thanks. I'll try." She wondered how she could assure being safe when, she knew, she was setting out impetuously, and the article interested her less than the possibility of finding some sort of clue to who killed Giulio, something dropped on the trail, some tiny bit of evidence the police may have missed.

She set the cup on the counter, nodded to Leo and walked to the door. Just as she stepped out, another woman, her head tilted against the morning breeze and securing a broad-brimmed hat on her head with one hand, bumped into her.

"Sorry." Leah jumped aside, apologizing.

The other woman grunted, and Leah hurried on her way.

In the field, just at the opening of the via cava, where, in an abrupt change from the flat adjoining field, the trail cut into a deep slice of rock, another flock of sheep was grazing in the wet grass. One little lamb was butting against its mother's teats, ready to feed. The mother placidly continued to graze, as if oblivious to the minor battle under her belly. The scene reminded Leah of Sara as a baby, greedily nursing.

"Oh, no!" she exclaimed aloud, remembering Sara's coming visit—perhaps too soon.

Leah shook her head. This was the story of her life. Always in a hurry, always distracted, always something intervening, so that she felt as if she were compelled to move at one hundred miles an hour in a dozen different directions. She sighed and passed under the glassed-in figure of San Antonio embedded in the rock overhang at the entrance to the trail. Within a few steps, she was enshrouded in the dusky light between the towering walls.

Ascending, she passed through the deep, narrow slits of rock to open spaces where the stone of the via cava glistened in the morning light. In these small plots of earth where the rock walls opened out there was a sheen of dew across the delicate grasses and weeds, and Leah could look out at the gorge. Languid clouds glided upward through the trees, slowly dissipating as the sun crept over the eastern horizon.

This walk was different for Leah than the one just two days ago. Fear nagged at the back of her mind and in her muscles, but at the same time, she felt in control. That someone had tried to kill her had not only frightened her, it had made her more angry than she had ever been and the anger strengthened her resolve. She was furious at some deep, visceral level that the killer had tried to harm her, and she now wanted not safety, but revenge.

Though the rock pathway was still damp, it had dried enough for Leah to feel the grip of her running shoes against the stone. She moved upward with a rhythmic pace, at times brushing the sides of the walls with her hands, just for the pleasure of feeling the rough texture. Ahead of her, at a bend in the trail, a clump of flowering cyclamen had burst out of a crack in the sheer wall, like the flowers she had seen the day of the murder. She stopped to bend down and put her face to the flowers. The blossoms were a deep crimson, thick and velvety, not as large as the commercial ones, but more real, more beautiful in their sturdy wildness. She thought for a moment of picking them, to take back to Nick, but decided against it; she still had far to go and they would be wilted by the time she got home.

And besides, why would I want to kill the most beautiful thing I've seen yet today? She hurried on toward the table rock.

Chapter Nineteen

Nick woke with a start. The workmen who were refurbishing the house adjacent, up the hill, were hammering on something. He yelled at the walls and ceiling. "Damn it! Can't a person get any sleep?"

He looked at the clock on his nightstand and turned toward Leah, who wasn't there.

"Leah!" he called into the outer room. "Bang on the ceiling, would you? Maybe those guys will stop." As soon as he said it, he realized it was an absurd suggestion. The workmen were in another house and would not hear her.

She didn't answer.

"Leah?"

Nick rose, slipped on his robe, fumbled into his

slippers, and went to find her. The other room was empty.

"Not again!"

He rushed back into the bedroom to get his clothes.

Chapter Twenty

Toward the top of the via cava, on a high ledge above the trail, a figure, dressed in dark clothes, face obscured by a turtle-necked sweater and a hat, held a rifle and crouched in the vines at the lip of the sheer wall.

Below, Leah quickened her pace. She was breathing heavily now, nearing the top.

The sensation of sudden wind near Leah's cheek was followed by the loud crack of a rifle. Her first response was to raise her arms and cover her head, thinking it must be falling rock. The first bullet missed; the second took her in the left arm. It cracked the humerus and opened a hole in the underflesh three inches above the elbow.

Leah dropped to the ground. She felt no pain. Gazing upward, the walls of the via cava seemed to lean inward,

157

as if they were closing over her. She noted a movement in the brush above, a figure. The sky appeared infinitely far away, the blue of first light, darkening. *A storm must be coming.* As she thought the words, the pain took hold in her arm and she turned her head to see blood seeping through her jacket onto the rocks.

"I've cut myself," she mumbled just before she blacked out.

Above her, the figure looked down, saw the blood darkening the rock at her side, and, crouching low, hurried back through the brush toward the road, laughing. "Idiot!"

Chapter Twenty-one

Secondo pulled the blanket close around his shoulders and neck. The day was warm enough, but in the shadow of the via cava, it was damp and chill. The cold from the long night on the bench had seeped through his blanket and the three layers of summer clothes he had scavenged from the town dump. He moved at a quick pace. He had not eaten since late morning the day before, and the caffeine and carbohydrates of the coffee and brioche coursed straight through his system, leaving him energized, at least for an hour or two. It felt good.

For years after his first manic incident in his early twenties, Secondo resisted the truth of his illness. His spending sprees ruined his mother financially. He rarely slept, and he cajoled as many women as he could into his bed. His friends laughed at his antics and he raced through the days oblivious to the trail of sadness behind him.

Then, one late autumn day on a walk up one of the vie cave, he had scaled a steep slope, up ten meters to the top, convinced he could leap to the other side of the trail.

After the fall, Secondo spent two months in the hospital. "An accident," his mother explained to the doctor. "An accident." She coaxed him into taking the medicine, and once he had, he was able to see his own acts clearly. Every day he lived with the shame of that foolish jump and what it had cost his mother. Within a few weeks, his mania degenerated into depression.

Secondo had grown up in the town and the forests and the vie cave, and the townspeople helped him when they could, seeing that he helped himself whenever he could summon the energy. As long as she was alive, his mother cared for him, forgiving him for stealing petty cash from her purse, doling out the pills when the stream of his blood reversed in his veins and hypomania—or worse, mania itself—again compelled him to frenetic days and sleepless nights. She watched her son. The illness dogged him relentlessly, turning the world gray in depression, and then spinning him like a leaf into mania.

She did not subject him to the embarrassment of seeing a psychiatrist because she knew the ingrained fear and shame some in the community felt toward mental illness. So, she traveled by herself to Rome, where no one knew them, and arranged with a doctor there for medication, which she kept secreted away from any prying eyes. Many in town knew that Secondo had mental problems, but the good among them colluded in the fiction that Secondo's mother had attempted to create, and kept an eye out for him.

The years before his mother's death, Secondo, under treatment, improved. One day, before she died, his mother went to her friend, Marcella, and told her she had arranged for Secondo's medication to be sent to her. Then she went home and told Secondo he would soon be getting his medicine from Marcella. She entreated Secondo to take it regularly.

"Do as I ask, Secondo. You are much better now, you see. It's the medicine that's helping you, and Marcella will make sure you get it, but she can't force you to take; you'll have to do that on your own because soon I won't be here to help you. I've made a calendar to remind you." Her eyes were tearing as she spoke and so, too, were Secondo's. "Do it for me, son, and for yourself. Nobody else but Marcella needs to know. They'll just assume you're as you have been these past few years. And Marcella won't say anything."

Then she died and Secondo was alone.

He honored his mother's request. On his own resources, after years of resisting, he watched the calendar every day and took the medicine, and though he tried to banish the hope from his mind, feeling more capable now, Secondo fantasized at times about having a real job as a street sweeper. As he walked upward, along the trail, he imagined himself with the long broom handle in his hands, the twigs of the broom curved from the sweeping motion: Back and forth, back and forth, along Via Vezzosa.

Secondo's revelry was broken by the report of a rifle.

Chapter Twenty-two

Nick stood outside the door of the police station, gulping air from the exertion of the run up the hill. He straightened his jacket and shook his hands loose at his sides, taking a few more breaths to calm himself before he entered, aware that if Signorina MacCleod saw that he was disheveled or out of breath she would know something was wrong and within minutes the news would be broadcast throughout the town. Drawing in one last, deep breath, he pressed the door handle and entered.

The Signorina, flaming hair floating in a wide sweep around her head, looked up from the yellow-covered mystery she was reading, making no attempt to disguise the fact that she was squandering the public's money on time spent reading detective stories. Her greeting was particularly perky.

"Good morning, Signor Contarini. You're up early this morning. Didn't finish your visa yesterday?"

"No. No I didn't. Is the lieutenant in?"

"For a few minutes. Giulio's death, you know." She stared at him as if she expected him to say something about the death, and he wondered if she knew that he and Leah had not come just about visas.

"I imagine he *is* very busy, but may I . . ."

"One minute." She smiled at him. "I'll see if he can see you."

She rose and walked slowly, languidly to the door of the inner office, her hips swinging like a slow pendulum under her tight gray skirt that fell just above the knees. Her high-heeled boots clicked with each step across the stone floor. At the lieutenant's door, she knocked lightly, and hearing the response, opened the door and leaned in. "The American is here."

After an instant, she turned back to Nick, looking at him quizzically, and motioned him in. He brushed by her, and she closed the door with a swift snap behind him.

"She what?"

"I think she's gone back up the via cava."

"Foolish, foolish woman!" Lieutenant Cavour's face reddened under his olive skin.

"At the moment, I agree with you, Lieutenant, and that's why I came to you rather than simply going after her myself. I'd like to go with you, please, because perhaps another stern warning from us both at the same time will do some good."

Cavour rubbed his forehead with his hand, shaking his head, his eyes closed. "Santa Madonna." He raised his head to Nick. "Your wife, Signor, is a great deal of trouble and I have too much already, but I suppose, yes, I must go with the hope that this last time, she will listen and let me do my work without interference."

"Have you been able to bring up the picture yet that Leah gave you?"

Cavour heard what Nick said, but let it pass as if he had not. Montaro had been working on bringing up the photo for hours, but was unsuccessful. He was still at work on it in the next room. "Well, there's nothing for it. We'll have to go find her. I'm assuming that under the guise of taking photos, she went back to the table rock?"

"She didn't take her camera this time. I think she just went back to look for clues that might have been missed."

"Ahhhh!" Cavour signaled Nick with a brusque wave of his hand to follow.

In the police car, Cavour vented his anger at Nick. "I wish you could control you wife!"

"Can you control yours?"

The lieutenant squirmed. "That's not the point." He rushed on before Nick could press the issue. "I don't have time to chase up and down the vie cave to take care of silly women who can't mind their own business."

"The vie cave *is* her business . . . I mean, the article."

"The article! The article! Not clues for the police! She's headstrong and she's looking for clues, not working on her article. You said it yourself. I wish both of you would stay put. You muddy the waters and steal our time, time when we could be working."

Nick tried to change the subject. "Who could have known something like this would happen in such a small town?"

"Don't try to change the subject." Distracted, Cavour had taken the curve in the road too fast and was forced to slam on the brakes and then accelerate again as a car behind him closed in on them. "And what? Do you think people in small towns don't suffer the same hatreds and angers like people in New York? You think we're all just nice boring people who never have problems or passions?"

"I didn't say that." Steadying himself with both hands on the dashboard, Nick turned to look at the lieutenant.

"Okay, okay. I know you didn't say it. Forgive me. You two have been good citizens, and I know you love it here, like the rest of us. We do have troubles here, but it's been decades since there's been murder." Suddenly pensive, he shook his head from side to side. "I just can't figure out why anyone would want to kill Giulio or Luisa."

Chapter Twenty-three

L eah lay unconscious in the middle of the trail, as if she had simply fallen gently backward, arms crooked, shoulder high. On the left side, blood was seeping onto the stone, pooling slowly in one of the little depressions made by the donkeys' hooves. Afraid to touch her, Secondo bent and looked closely, but still could not tell if the blood was coming from her side or from her arm. It appeared to be from the chest, the heart.

"Oh, mama!" He stood and looked around him, then lifted his gaze upward. No one. A stream of sweat dripped into his eyes, and he swiped his arm across his brow and shuffled his feet, uncertain what to do. "My God!"

He looked up again, then knelt carefully beside Leah and lifted the edge of her sleeve. It was the arm that was bleeding. He looked around. No one. He looked back at Leah's arm and shook his head frantically back and forth, then stopped and unbuttoned his outer shirt, grabbed a stick and poked at the shirt until he made a tear large enough to put his fingers through just below the neck line. With a sudden jerk he ripped a broad strip of material free of the shirt.

Secondo strained to remember what his mother had said when he watched her once put a tourniquet on Marcella. The woman had cut her upper arm to the bone on a sharp wire while she was climbing through the fence of her little sheep pen near the river. Secondo and his mother, on their way to picnic in the shade along the water, found her, and Secondo's mother had bound Marcella's arm, while Secondo watched. Now he talked himself into it.

"Not too thin. If it's too thin it will damage the tissue and be too tight.

"Put it between the cut and the heart.

"Now under the arm and on top a square knot.

"Now a stick through the loop of the knot.

"Now a twist and a twist, but gentle, not too tight."

Hands trembling, he gently eased the cloth under Leah's upper arm, tied a knot, slipped the stick through and then twisted, until he saw the blood diminish. Checking to make sure the tourniquet was not too tight, he wrapped the loose ends of the strip of cloth around the stick and tucked the ends gently into the strap around her arms so the tourniquet would hold.

When he had finished, Secondo stood and looked again up and down the trail as if help might appear. He sucked a sudden deep breath, reached down, and scooped Leah up in his arms.

"I'm doing this," he said to the air, grunting as he lifted her. "I'm doing this myself."

Adjusting her on his lifted knee, he turned down trail, stepping carefully, gently. She was light, but before long he was sweating profusely under the limp weight and had to stop every few paces to raise his knee and rebalance her on his thigh while he righted his grip under her arms and legs. Moving downward, the weight seemed to increase. It took all of Secondo's tenuous strength to hold her and to fight the gravity of the descent.

When he reached the spot where he had dropped his blanket, he laid Leah down gently in the middle and wrapped her in it. She was pale, and he knew that the loss of blood had made her cold, even if she couldn't feel it—just like it had Marcella. He raised her again and continued down the via cava, heel first against the stone, then rolling carefully forward, so intent on his footing that when he rounded the last turn before the cava opened out into the field, he did not see Cavour and Nick coming along the field's edge. When he did see them, he stopped abruptly, just as Nick looked up.

"Oh my God! What have you done?"

Cavour grabbed Nick's arm before he could break free. "Stop, Nick. I'll handle it. "Secondo, stop!"

"I am stopped."

The two men sprinted to Secondo, and beside him the lieutenant turned his head to hide a faint smile. "Yes, you are, and now we're here."

Hands trembling, Nick gently pulled back the blanket, which had fallen over Leah's face. She was still unconscious, her skin alabaster white, cold to his touch. He leaned his ear close to her mouth and nose; her breath burst in faint puffs against his cheek. "She's alive!" He emitted a sudden loud gasp, tears pouring from his eyes, and he eased his arms under her to take her from Secondo.

Secondo stared at him, yielding her to Nick. "I put on a tourniquet. Somebody shot her in the arm."

"Take her legs, Secondo. I'll hold her shoulders."

Though Secondo had been even-tempered for over two years now, others had heard the gossip and even the townspeople had imprisoned the memory of his past behavior in their minds and in that way refused to let him improve. They remained wary, perpetually unsure of his state of mind. He had come to accept it, but at this moment it frustrated him to tears.

"Stop crying, Secondo! There's no time. Just help him get her in the car. You've done a good job."

"I know I did! I know it!" His voice carried all the pent-up anger of the stigmatized.

Cavour, who had turned toward the car, stopped in surprise and jerked his head around to look at Secondo, who was holding Leah's legs. In the years he had known

Secondo, the lieutenant could not remember him seeming that normal, and he flushed at how condescending the words "You've done a good job" must have sounded to the man who had rescued Leah.

Chapter Twenty-four

"I've got her now, Secondo."

Nick shifted to slide his arm under Leah's legs and take her full weight on his own. He rested her against the back door of the car as Secondo reached to open the door, then turned sideways and, moving carefully, bent and stepped into the car. Secondo shut the door behind him, and Lieutenant Cavour started the motor.

Secondo sat quietly in the front seat, glancing into the rearview mirror to watch Nick cradling Leah. Over the years as Nick and Leah returned regularly to Scansansiano, Secondo had fallen a little in love with Leah, but he knew she was afraid of him because of the way he acted. Her fears of him, he thought, must be similar to his fears for himself: When would the illness strike? What would he do when it did?

172

He had never done anything to anyone but himself physically, and he was thankful the others appeared to trust he never would. Years before, on a whim, he had stolen money from Signora Carlotta, and she had beaten him with a broom for doing it, and then he threatened her with a stick, but she said she would not tell if he gave the money back, and he did, and she never told. He hoped others, especially Leah, didn't know these things, but maybe there were too many things and there was too much gossip: the Lieutenant himself had caught him on the park bench having hallucinations and the old man that lived above the piazza had seen him that day too.

He looked in the rearview mirror again. Leah's head hung back over Nick's forearm.

"Secondo, after the hospital you'll need to come to the station to make a statement." Cavour was taking the curve very fast and when Secondo glanced again in the mirror, he saw Nick leaning with the weight of Leah in his arms.

Nick hissed from the back, "Take it easy. I can barely hold her as it is."

"Sorry."

Secondo had considered that he would need to make a statement. "Of course I will. That's what witnesses and the police do."

Chapter Twenty-five

Speeding up the hill toward the hospital in the new part of town, the two-way radio emitted a burst of static. "Montaro to Lieutenant. Come in Lieutenant."

Lieutenant Cavour reached to lift the speaker from its hook and flipped a switch on the side, imagining the rotund, bald-headed computer specialist sitting in front of the radio, grasping the speaker in his beefy fingers. He liked Montaro, his ready laugh and gentle nature, but most of all he appreciated the man's computer skills and he relied on Montaro for all but the easiest functions when it came to details of a crime. Signorina MacCleod he would never trust with such details.

"Here, Montaro. What is it?"

"The picture. Just to let you know, I can bring it up

now. It's been a real bear to work with. Something about the interface."

"Okay Montaro, just give me the essentials."

"I'm having trouble enlarging it. So far just the two men. The killer mostly has his back to the camera. You can only see an outline of his face and the hat covers his hair and appears to cast a shadow over most of the face, though it's difficult to say exactly if it's all shadow because it's just so small a photo. Things could be clearer when we enlarge it."

"Good work, Montaro. Keep at it."

"Don't expect too much. It might be fuzzy when it does come up."

"Do what you can."

"Okay. Out." Montaro was glad to ring off. The lieutenant sounded unusually grumpy.

Cavour slammed the receiver back on it's hook.

In the back seat, Nick adjusted his leg and spoke in a loud whisper, "I thought you were familiar with the computer?"

Cavour squirmed. "I am. For the basic things. I assumed bringing up the photos would be easy. Anyway, Montaro is good and he'll get the rest of it figured out."

Nick looked down at Leah and spoke with barely controlled anger. "Soon, I hope."

The hospital stood on a hill on the far side of town, one of the last buildings before the countryside. It was a large, rectangular structure three stories high with windows spaced like soldiers along the length of it. At one time, the outer walls had been painted bright white with a blue trim that sparkled in the sunshine, but that was long before the war, and when the Lieutenant pulled carefully into the emergency lane, Nick noticed, as he had not noticed before—in the odd way one sees detail in sharp relief during trauma—that the paint was chipped and the trim faded to a dull gray.

Easing to a stop at the emergency room, Cavour flung the driver's door wide, and ran ahead while Nick struggled to lift Leah out of the back seat without hurting her.

Secondo had jumped from the front seat to stretch out his hands to help.

"It's okay, Secondo. I've got her. You get the door."

Unable to brush away the sweat and tears from his face, Nick hunched his shoulder to wipe the drops from his ears, sniffed at the drips coming from his nose, and turned sideways and edged through the door that Secondo held open on one side and Cavour on the other.

Cavour went to the desk and the nurse on duty. He had already alerted her that they were coming, and the nurse ushered Nick into one of the side areas, drawing the curtain behind him. Nick, with the last of his strength, laid Leah gently on the high bed.

Blood seeped onto the sheets from her wound. Nick sucked air, his heart pounding. He was sweating profusely, and the tears were streaming down his cheeks. He reached for a corner of the sheet to wipe his face.

The nurse had clipped away the bandage and was looking at the wound. "Be calm. Don't worry. She does have a bad wound, but whoever put this tourniquet on her arm did a good job. Otherwise she would have bled to death."

Hearing a step behind him, Nick turned. Secondo had entered the curtained area quietly and was standing just behind him.

"I saw my mother do it once. And I saw it again on one of those TV doctor shows from America."

Nick managed a weak smile. "That's at least one good thing from America then, but I imagine your mother was a better teacher."

Secondo shook his head. "She was, but the nature shows are good too."

Chapter Twenty-six

Leah woke a few minutes before noon. She opened her eyes and without moving her head glanced around the room. She stuck out her tongue to wet her lips, but her mouth was dry. Her left arm ached. She raised her eyes, following the tube from the crook of one elbow to the top of the stand where the morphine drip was next to the bed. Turning her head slightly she could see a second tube, for hydration.

When she spoke, the words came out as a mumble. She puckered her lips trying to force moisture forward from her throat.

At the sound of her voice, Nick jumped from his chair, where he had been dozing, took the water glass from the stand, and held the straw to Leah's mouth. She drank with effort. When she spoke again, it was one word only.

"Nick?"

He seemed to be standing far above her. She struggled to focus on his face, but it made her woozy.

"Pan!" she blurted with a force that suprised both Nick and the nurse who had just entered the room.

"Well, that's a good sign," the nurse remarked matter of factly.

Nick held the cup to Leah's mouth. Lifting her head barely above the pillow, she vomited, and then cried out in pain when the retching jostled her arm. The waves of nausea subsided, and breathing as deeply as she dared, she lay back on her pillow. Nick wiped the edges of her mouth and raised the water to her lips once again, at the same time taking a second sputum cup from the bedside tray. He held the cup close to her lips.

"Here, spit the first sip out and then I'll give you some clean water to drink."

When they were done, she stared at Nick, whispering, "What happened?"

Seeing her innocent look, Nick struggled with the anger that had replaced his relief in hearing her speak, in seeing her eyes open. "Someone shot you."

"Shot me?"

"You're stubborn, Leah, and if we can't catch him first, this guy will do what he needs to kill you. From now on, you've got to listen to me and the Lieutenant. You've *got* to."

Even now in Leah's disoriented state, Nick knew her impetuous anger was filtering through the medication in little blips of feeling she couldn't articulate. Nick loved her for this feisty, independent spirit, and yet at the same time he recognized that it too often catapulted her into serious trouble, and he wanted to be able to stop her from hurting herself, while leaving her free-spirited. She had never understood this.

Still, at the moment his face was shriveled from worry, and she let her compassion for him negate her own frustration. This was the way of their wildly incompatible passion. Her courage was impetuous, his consistent, long lasting. Her work—and her love—came in spurts of intense energy, his in the way of constant, methodical and daily practice.

"I'm sorry, Nick." She meant for his suffering.

"I am too." He meant for her pain. And when he took her right hand gently in his own and shook his head slowly, sadly, he willed his words to mean that he wanted her safe, he wanted to live with her for the rest of his life, he wanted her to be alive.

"Leah, you've got to let this go. Let the Lieutenant deal with it. Whoever it is really will kill you, don't you see that? He'll chase you down, and kill you because he thinks you can identify him as Giulio's killer."

Saying "Lieutenant" conjured the man himself. Lieutenant Cavour parted the curtains and came to stand by Nick at Leah's bed. He looked down at her with a stern face.

"You are an irresponsible woman, Signora. And you cause me trouble I don't need. It's a wonder you're still alive. If Secondo hadn't found you, and applied the tourniquet . . ."

"Secondo?" Her eyebrows lifted in suprise.

"Yes. He followed you up the trail and came running when he heard the shot. When he saw the wound was your arm, he fashioned a tourniquet out of a stick and part of his shirt. You're lucky, very lucky, though I don't know why he was following you."

Leah's face twisted with the effort of speech. "I saw him on the bench."

Nick explained. "He told me. He took the money you gave him and went to get coffee. After you left, Sabina was talking about you in the bar to everyone as they came in, so he knew you were going up the via cava."

"But everyone in town already knows I'm writing the article."

"And given Sabina, everyone who drinks coffee in the morning, knew that you had gone up there today." Cavour shook his head, frustrated. "So, it wouldn't be much for anyone willing to put their mind to it, to guess that since you're always up on the trails, and you were up there today . . ."

"Okay, somebody's made a good guess that it was me that saw Giulio being pushed off the cliff, but how could they know for certain? And anyway, I've seen other people up on the trail."

"But I doubt very many. And whoever was guessing it seems guessed correctly, unless there is some other reason for someone to kill you?"

Leah laughed, then winced in pain. She was suprised to realize it was a real question.

"No, of course not. What would it be? Who cares if I write about the vie cave? They've been written about before, dozens of times. And that's all I'm doing here."

"Not all. You're seeing things. And after Giulio's and then Signora Luisa's death, I'm not sure the killer is reasonable—except in his own convoluted way. I just don't know. But I have to think of all possibilities, and since you've been working on this article, people are dying."

Leah turned her head to the wall. "Let me sleep. It has nothing to do with my article, but somehow everything to do with that cantina."

Cavour hunched his shoulders at Nick, turned, and walked out through the slit in the curtains.

Leah opened her eyes and turned back to Nick. "Good riddance." But she had moved too quickly, and cried out in pain.

When the nurse parted the curtains, carrying the little paper cup with sleeping pills, Leah extended her good arm and took the glass of water from the nightstand. The nurse adjusted the IV and left as quietly as she had come in.

Nick leaned to kiss Leah on the forehead and sat in the chair beside the bed. "Sleep, Leah. You need it."

Within a few minutes Leah was sleeping soundly, drugged and dreamless.

Chapter Twenty-seven

When Leah woke the next morning, Nick was sitting beside her.

"Have you been here all night?" With effort, she turned toward him, wincing as she did.

"Yeah." He waved his hand in the air as if sitting in the chair all night was unimportant. "Still a lot of pain, isn't there. I'm sorry."

"Oh, it'll get better."

The nurse came through the curtains, and laid a syringe on the nightstand. "Of course you'll get better." She put her hand on Leah's forehead, and Leah shrank from her touch. The nurse's manner was uncomfortably familiar.

"Time for more morphine." The nurse picked up the

syringe from the stand and inserted it into a port on the tube leading to Leah's arm.

"I don't feel like I need more just yet. It hurts, but not that badly."

"Better to anticipate, otherwise when it starts to hurt badly, you'll be sorry."

"I think I can stand it."

"Just let me decide." The nurse's smile was condescending, smarmy, as if she were addressing a little girl. It made Leah shudder.

When the nurse stepped away, Leah turned to Nick and spoke in a loud whisper, "I don't like her; there's something funny about her."

As the words were out of her mouth, Leah noticed the nurse's feet just below the curtain. She glanced at Nick and raised her index finger to her mouth with her good hand, then took it away to point at the feet, mouthing, "I hope she doesn't speak English." In the silence, the nurse turned and tiptoed away.

An aide brought Leah's breakfast, and Nick smuggled in a croissant from the bar in the piazza to add to the distasteful-looking gruel, but the morphine had dampened Leah's hunger, and she nibbled without interest at the pastry, after she pushed the bowl of mush aside.

"I can't figure this out, Nick. It made sense to come after me just after the murder, but why now? Surely the killer knows that if I had a picture, I would have given it to the police by now and killing me wouldn't do any good. And if I didn't get a picture and didn't know who the murderer was—which if I had, would have been common knowledge by now—then there's no need to kill me. Right?"

As serious as her words were, Nick smiled. Her speech was slow, drawn to inordinate length by the morphine, but it made sense.

"I don't know either. Maybe whoever it is just wants to kill you."

"Just because I'm me?"

"Yeah."

"You can't be serious."

"No, I'm probably not. It just came into my mind, but nothing else makes sense."

"Let's go over the possibilities again. It seems—"

"May we come in?" It was Anna's voice.

"Of course." Nick rose to his feet and reached to part the curtain. He embraced each one of the Antoninis and they stepped in to bend and embrace Leah.

"Oh, Leah." Anna's voice trembled with emotion. "We're so sorry. We knew the evening of the Befania that something was wrong. I wish I had encouraged you to speak more openly, maybe we could have prevented this."

"I don't think so. And I didn't want to say anything—we were afraid to get you involved."

"But we're your friends . . ."

The nurse appeared through the curtains. "So many visitors! Too many. You need to rest, Signora." She stared at the Antoninis. "Just a few more minutes, please."

After the nurse left, Leah shook her head. "That nurse. She hovers over me like a mother duck, she seems very strange."

Leonardo chuckled. "She is strange. She's Giulio's cousin, didn't you know?"

"No! She never said, and no one told me."

"There's some trouble in the family about the inheritance. She and Giulio were at odds about it, but I don't think she was ever a candidate to inherit."

"I'm getting more confused by the minute about all this."

"Yes. Confusing. It sounds like we'd better get out of here now, or the nurse'll be after us." They bent again to hug her and left quietly through the parted curtain.

Leah sighed heavily. "Nick, do you think it makes a difference that it's Giulio's cousin who's taking care of me? I mean could she have done it?"

"Don't let your imagination run away with you. The Antoninis would have alerted us if they felt that anything was wrong with her, and they would know better than we do. Just try to get some sleep. I'm going to get coffee. I'll back back in a few minutes."

Chapter Twenty-eight

Later that day, Montaro stepped through the curtains surrounding Leah's bed. She was asleep, and Nick, half asleep himself, turned, startled. Seeing Montaro, he brought his index finger to his lips, and in the same instant noticed Montaro held a photo. Nick whispered, "You got it enlarged?

Montara nodded and smiled, whispering back, "I was just going to show the Lieutenant. I thought he was here." He held the photo close to his chest, as if to protect it from Nick.

"He was, just a little while ago. I think he went for coffee. Can I see it?" Nick motioned for them to step out through the curtains into the hallway.

Montaro followed and stood in front of Nick with the photo still held to his chest.

"It's okay, Montaro. We're in this up to our necks anyway, so what can it hurt? And Leah's the one that's suffering for it."

"No, the Lieutenant should be first . . . and he'll be very angry if he isn't, but you can come with me. If he's not here, then he's probably out and about somewhere."

"He's angry already, and it won't make a difference if we see it, because he's going to see it within a few minutes and he'll be the one to act, right?"

Nick reached for it but Montaro drew back. "No! First the Lieutenant."

"Oh, all right! Let's go find him." Nick glanced at Leah—she was sleeping soundly, and he motioned Montaro into the hallway with a brisk wave of his hand.

As he bounded down the stairwell steps, he called back over his shoulder to Montaro, "Could you see who it was?"

"After we talk to the lieutenant." Awkward on the steps, Montaro scurried after him as best he could.

Nick shook his head. "My God you're persistent."

They rushed out the back way, and ran down the street. It was market day. The piazza was crowded with early morning shoppers weighed down by heavy sacks of groceries, celery, and brown-crusted Tuscan bread sticking out of the tops of the sacks. Housewives, young and old, pulled their rolling grocery bags slowly across the cobblestones.

Nick and Montaro darted among the shoppers,

brushing shoulders with some, who yelled after them, "Idiots! Watch where you're going!"

Nick spotted Lieutenant Cavour in the corner of the piazza near the bar, talking to a group of the older men who were sitting at a table in the sun, protected by a stone wall from the gentle but cold breeze. They were drinking coffee and laughing over a joke one of them had just told.

As Nick approached the center of the piazza, he heard someone call out, "Papa!" Nick jerked to a stop and turned. From the side road coming into the piazza, Sara and Jonathan were running toward him. Montaro veered to the right just in time to avoid colliding with Nick from behind.

"What are *you two* doing here!" Nick said gruffly.

Sara stopped short and Jonathan plowed into her from behind almost knocking her over. She straightened herself, then stomped her foot and yelled at him, and Nick remembered how as a little girl she had done the same thing when her anger flared.

"Fine welcome! I haven't seen you in months and you want to know what I'm doing here? I told you we were coming. I talked to Mom on the phone!"

Montaro, who understood no English, was tugging at Nick's sleeve and motioning toward the Lieutenant. Nick turned his head back and forth from Cavour to Sara. "Sorry. I'm sorry. Come here."

They moved toward each other, pulling away from

the few who had gathered to watch Nick argue with this new couple.

Coming close to Sara, Nick whispered, "Listen, I have to speak fast and you have to listen carefully and not talk right now. Your mother has been shot—"

"What?" Both Sara and Jonathan drew in a sharp breath.

"She's okay, she's okay. Don't make a show of it. Just try to keep calm. It's an arm wound, and she's fine, but I think we know who did it and I'm going over to the Lieutenant just now."

Nick nodded in the direction of the table where the men were sitting, watching them.

"We've got a photo. So come with me, but keep quiet. We've got to work fast."

Sara took his arm. "But wait Dad, where's Mamma? I want to see her."

Nick reached to touch her cheek, moved by Sara's use of Mamma as she had called Leah when she was a little girl.

Montaro took his sleeve again. "Signor, the Lieutenant."

"But where is she? And who's this guy?"

"She's in the hospital. I'll take you there as soon as I talk to the lieutenant. And this is Sergeant Montaro."

Sara opened her mouth to say something else, but Nick raised his hands, spread flat, to stop her and barked, "Not now! What your mother most needs is for us to find the one who shot her. I'll explain everything later."

He turned and rushed on across the piazza. Sara, Jonathan, and Montaro dashed after him, Sara crying as she ran. Jonathan ran beside her holding her hand. "Don't cry. Just listen to your dad. He said it's an arm wound, and we'll see her soon."

The men at the table, including the lieutenant, had been watching them, amused by the shouting in English. They rarely saw foreigners, especially Americans, argue—to them, Americans were insipid, nothing like Italians—and the men wondered who these new people were.

Seeing the look on Nick's face as he came closer, Cavour stood. "What is it? Is the Signora worse? And who are these two?"

Nick was panting. He ignored Cavour's questions and motioned toward the photo Montaro was holding. When Cavour took it, Nick bent and looked at it. "My God, it looks like Italo!"

Cavour was holding the photo close to his face, squinting.

Nick rushed on. "The hat. Look at the hat. I know it's Italo's. I saw it in the back seat of his car and he was bragging about it. And the tassles. I saw them in his car. Who else has tassles like that? Or a hat that expensive?"

"Calm yourself, signor. Many people have these cowboy hats."

"But not this expensive, and not with those tassles."

"No, but you can buy those tassles, you know." Cavour rubbed his chin. "At any rate we'd better find

Italo. And you'd better tell me who these two people are."

"My daughter and her fiancé." Nick ignored formal introductions, but Cavour, imbued with centuries of the grace of his ancestors, extended his hand. "It's a pleasure to meet you. I'm sorry it's in such circumstances."

Sara and Jonathan returned his handshake, and spoke at the same time: "Who's Italo?"

Secondo had come up from behind. He was curious about the two new Americans, but had overheard the mention of Italo's name. "You're looking for Italo? I just saw him going into the back entrance of the hospital."

Nick paled. "Are you sure it was him?

"I think so. I was a ways down the block, but the man was dressed like him.

"My God!" Nick and Cavour sprinted back toward the hospital, but Enrico, one of the men at the table, called out.

"Stop Lieutenant! It's not Italo."

Nick and the Lieutenant stopped and turned.

Enrico motioned to them to return. "It couldn't have been Italo. I saw him just fifteen minutes ago. He was down the gorge on the river fishing, so I stopped the car to chat with him. He was on foot, and he couldn't possibly have gotten back up the hill and to the hospital in that short of a time. He's in good shape, but no one on foot could cover five kilometers in fifteen minutes time." He laughed at the absurdity of it.

Chapter Twenty-nine

It took a moment for Leah's waking eyes to focus. Unaccustomed to drugs as she was, she could see only a fuzzy outline at the bottom of the bed. She rubbed her eyes with her right hand, and then squinted, straining to see who it was. The face came into focus.

"Oh! Hi. I'm suprised to see you." A dull recollection of their uncomfortable interchange at the Befania dinner flitted across her mind. "It's nice of you to come. I thought you had left town after Signora Seta . . ."

"What? Was murdered? No. We didn't leave, though we thought we were going to. We decided it was just too late and had been too upsetting, so we stayed on at a bed and breakfast outside of town."

"Probably a better idea. How did you know I was here?"

"A little bird told me."

"A little bird?" Leah was fully awake now, her heart pounding.

"Yes, sweetie. The woods above the via cava are full of them, don't you know? You do know all the vie cave well, don't you. And you see, after, I bushwhacked a ways and then dropped onto the via cava and went up trail and around by car down the road. When I saw the lieutenant and your dear sweet husband and that idiot Secondo loading you into the car I . . ." the voice turned to a deeper singsong. "At the end of the game, sweetie, everyone goes into the sack, the king—or shall I say in this context, the American—as well as the pawn."

"You!"

"Yes, me. Surprised?"

"But why?"

"First the photo. I thought maybe you knew who it was, but then when you obviously didn't, I figured the photo was unclear, so now it's just you, and your stupid flirting with Italo."

"I never flirted with Italo!"

"The Befania dance at the Antoninis.'"

"That was—"

"That was what I know it was! He's mine! I saw the way he looked at you and brought out a chair for you at the cenone, but you'll never have him!" She had raised her voice, then caught herself.

"But Giulio's aunt?"

"You're desperate to delay the inevitable aren't you?" Angelina's eyes gleamed with a strange lust.

"Nurse." Leah tried to yell, but her voice was muted by the medication.

"They're with other patients and I've closed the door." A wild grin distorted her face. "No one can hear you, sweetie pie."

Leah watched her reach for the pillow on the chair where Nick had dropped it earlier that morning.

"It won't take long. But you can carry this thought with you." Angelina held the pillow by one hand and, smiling, fluffed it with the other as she spoke. "Giulio, his aunt . . . all of that is a long tale of love—more love than you could ever dream of or understand."

Her face turned dark. Her eyes widened in fury. "And an interfering wench like yourself just doesn't have any time or understanding to hear that tale."

Then, as suddenly as Angelina had turned angry, she reverted to a sickly sweet voice. "Take it like a woman, sweetie. It won't last long. The bell has sounded and it's useless to say no, so you may as well just give in to it."

She raised the pillow and stepped closer to the bed.

"Like . . . hell . . . I . . . will." Leah meant the words to be strong, but they only stumbled from her lips. With a cry of pain, she batted at the pillow, but it felt as if her arm was moving through molasses and she was too weak to fight for long. The smooth cloth of the pillow-case enveloped her face. She smelled the clean lemon scent of the laundry soap, even as she struck ever more weakly at the air, and, finally, knew only darkness.

Chapter Thirty

With Nick in the lead, Jonathan, Sara, Lieutenant Cavour, and Sergeant Montara bounded up the stairwell two at a time and burst through the doorway of Leah's room. Nick yanked open the curtains around her bed and hurled himself at Angelina, pulling her off Leah. Cavour, shouting at Montaro to bring the nurse, moved to help Nick and was restraining Angelina by one arm, as Nick held the other.

"Sara!" Nick yelled.

Sara darted to grab the pillow away from her mother's face. "Mamma! Mamma!" Her voice broke as she called out the words, and the tears streamed down her face. She leaned close, holding her cheek next to her mother's mouth to see if she could feel her breath. Jonathan stood behind her, holding her shoulders, whispering. "It will be all right. The nurse is coming. It's okay." He spoke even as he felt certain that Leah, unmoving and pale, was already gone.

Held by Cavour and Nick, Angelina quivered with fury, and fought to break free. "Italo should have it. It's his! His cantina! His restaurant! You stupid stupid fools, you don't know anything. Italo wants it!"

Cavour and Nick compelled her toward the doorway.

Two nurses brushed past them, shouting for Sara and Jonathan to move out of the way.

In the hallway, while Angelina screamed and kicked at them, Montaro cuffed her, and then, with the Lieutenant, led her away, still kicking and screaming.

Nick heard the echoes of her frenzied, anguished voice fading down the stairwell. "Damn you, you idiots! The cantina's Italo's. Giulio wouldn't give it to him. He wouldn't! It's Italo's! Italo's, you fools!"

Chapter Thirty-one

With quick, precise movements, the older nurse bent over Leah and slipped her fingers to the side of Leah's neck, searching for a heartbeat. "Barrier," she said quietly to the other nurse, who quickly pulled open the drawer on the bed stand and pulled out a plastic sheet with a cloth webbing in the center of it. While the older nurse attempted mouth to mouth and compressions, the younger nurse raced out and came back with a defibrillator. The current jolted Leah's body and with a cough and cry of pain, she started up and then fell back, moaning.

"Mamma!" Sara stepped toward the bed again, but the nurse pushed her away.

"Give her a minute. She's okay now, but you need to let her come back, to figure out where she is."

"But—"

"No." The nurse held Sara's arm. "Let her be!" Seeing Sara's eyes, her voice softened. "She's not going anywhere."

At the sound of Sara's voice, Leah opened her eyes. "Sara? Jonathan?"

Nick burst into the room from the hallway and nudged against the nurse to squeeze in and lean over Leah. He tried to speak, but his voice broke in staccato sobs.

"She's okay, Papa." Sara eased out of Jonathan's arms and embraced her father. "She's okay."

"Hi." Leah smiled weakly. "It was Angelina. I don't understand. And now here are Sara and Jonathan. And I don't understand that either." Her words were slurred.

"Don't try to understand, Mamma. Just rest and get well."

"This wasn't the way I envisioned it. I thought we'd go to Rome, to the airport." Leah's eyes had glazed, the lids heavy, and she strained to keep them open. Thickened by the dryness of her mouth, her words came slowly. With effort, she ran her tongue over her lips, trying to produce some moisture.

"We'll figure it out later, Leah. Just rest. Please." Nick touched her right shoulder gently.

"Yes." The nurse was emphatic. "Rest. And you all need to leave so she can do just that."

"I won't," Nick protested.

The older nurse who had given Leah CPR glared at him. "Do you want to lose her?"

"No. Of course not."

"Then come back in the evening."

"But I'm her husband."

"If you'd like to complain, I suggest you talk to my supervisor, who will be in in the morning. For now, I'm in charge."

She was a tall woman with arms like a wrestler and a commanding voice, but her eyes softened as she looked at him and the young couple looking at her. "Okay, three more minutes—and then you go."

Chapter Thirty-two

A few days later Italo sat on the edge of the chair in front of Lieutenant Cavour's desk. "The hat. She asked to borrow it. She said wearing my clothes"—he hesitated, fumbling, and hung his head—"turned her on."

"Turned her on?"

"A 'rush'—you know."

"No, I don't know. Why don't you tell me."

Italo smiled sheepishly. "She was always doing it— wearing my shirts when we were alone, that sort of thing. And I thought the hat was just the same thing. I swear to you, I didn't know anything about the other." He paused. "You don't . . . you don't think she did it on purpose to implicate me, do you?"

"I don't know. But it seems improbable that you

didn't know anything. You were with her, staying with her, how could you not know?"

"She's crazy, I tell you. She's obsessed with me and she was always doing odd stuff. Like I was a king or something. But she's nuts." He blushed.

"And you like that I suppose?"

Forgetting for a moment where he was, Italo grinned.

Cavour shook his head. "And what, signor, does your wife think of this obsession and your acquiesence to it?"

Italo's head jerked up. "I didn't know you knew. You won't tell her . . ."

"You told Signor Nick that she did know."

Italo blushed. "I . . . I was bragging a little."

"Ahh . . . I see."

"She doesn't know everything. Please, please don't tell her."

"Are you so naive? We know much more than most people think we know—because it's our business—and though you tell yourself your wife doesn't know everything, you should have learned by now that women are smarter than men. I think I can positively say that Angelina and your wife know about each other."

"But she's said nothing."

"Perhaps she's biding her time . . . at any rate I won't need to tell her. This afternoon we are releasing full details of the case to the press. It will all be on the news, and of course, we'll be checking your alibis, so the word will get round. The whole region will be buzzing."

"Please, does it have to be made public?"

"When the louse falls into the hopper, he thinks—for a while anyway—to be the miller." The Lieutenant laughed. "Yes, I'm afraid it does."

Italo whined. "Why?"

"Ah, Tiburzi the second cowed by his wife! I'm afraid that the word is already out. You've been with Angelina a long time, and you would have to be particularly oblivious to think no one understood your . . . ah . . . relationship."

"But I only presented her as a friend."

"Italo. Italo." Cavour shook his head. "Sometimes I am ashamed to be of the male gender. We can be so stupid in our egotism. I think the best thing you can do is to get the jump on the gossip and start buying your wife some very fine presents. And I mean diamonds, not chocolates!" He threw his head back and roared with laughter.

Italo rushed out of Cavour's office glancing backward, as if the lieutenant might be following him, and he slammed head-on into Nick, who had just stepped forward to open the door for Leah. Nick fell back against her and she let out a screech of pain at the blow to her arm. Both of them landed in a tangle on the floor with Italo, who landed on top of them.

"Good God, Italo, what the hell are you doing!?" Nick shoved him off, rolled over and got to his feet, extending his hand to help Leah, who was wincing with pain.

"Sorry, I'm sorry. I didn't mean to . . . I've got to go. I'm sorry." He rushed off red-faced to the street.

Leah was cradling her bad arm. Nick gently grasped her shoulders. "Are you okay?"

She groaned, wincing. "Damn it, it just hurts. What a donkey that guy is."

"And much subdued. He even apologized! Punishment is lame, but it arrives."

"You think his punishment is lame? Just wait until the whole mess is public. Even if his wife knew something before, she won't stand for it once it's in the papers, she'll shred him."

Inside, the secretary, her bright red hair bobbing above a tight, bright blue sweater, short black skirt and knee-high black boots, moved toward the Lieutenant's office.

Cavour came around the desk to greet them. "Ah, you're laughing. You must have run into Italo. He left in a great hurry—on his way to the jeweler's I imagine." A sly smile creased his dark, handsome face.

They shook hands, and Cavour motioned them to the chairs in front of his desk, then took his own seat.

Leah spoke first. "Thanks for seeing us. We wanted to find out what's going to happen now."

"Of course. Well, once we finish with the paperwork

this will go to the district judge. I believe the first thing that will happen is that the judge will issue orders to decide whether or not Angelina is competent to be tried. If she is, I imagine maybe even before she is formally charged, she will be offered what we call a quick trial."

"What's that?" Leah and Nick asked at the same time.

"I think you don't have it in America, I don't know." He put his hand to his forehead, as if trying to remember. "Anyway . . . it limits the number of witnesses and the kind of evidence that can be submitted, and if she's convicted, then it gives her only two-thirds of the usual sentence. And all the proceedings of a fast-track trial are closed to the public."

"And if she doesn't take it?"

"Well, maybe she won't take the option, and if she doesn't, it could be months and months before she's even indicted and after that, if the judge indicts her, it may take many more months."

"But she confessed."

"Yes, but that brings us back around to her mental capacity."

"But what about us? We can't stay for months and months."

"No, of course not. You're not expected to. We'll keep you informed and you will come back."

"What if we can't?"

"You'll find a way. You like us here, I think." He smiled warmly.

"But—"

"You've been here enough times now and for long enough so that you begin to see, how do you say, 'our warts and all.'"

Nick grunted. "I hope murder isn't a common occurrence here—a wart we just haven't noticed before?"

"Not that common, thankfully, but not as unusual as I would like. And remember, technically, Angelina, or for that matter, Italo, is not from here—they are not Scansansianese."

"Still, they seem to be here all the time, and integrated into the community." Leah was shaking her head.

"They're both from away. Didn't you get the whole saga of Tiburzi from Italo? Everyone else in Scansaniano has."

Nick guffawed. "He told me on the way to the Befania at the farmhouse south of town."

"He tells anyone that listens."

"So, at least it wasn't anyone from here . . . but I'm curious about two things—was it Italo's rifle? And what will happen to the cantina?"

"No, no one from here, thank God. And that's important to us. It would have been like discovering one of our family was a killer. And yes, it was his rifle, which he shouldn't have been carrying in the car. Angelina took it when she borrowed his car that day, to get quickly up behind the via cava, so she could be in position by the time Leah came along. All she had to do was hike back up to the road just above the cava, put the gun back, and drive back to town to be in the piazza where everyone could see her. As for the cantina, well, who knows? Bureaucracies move slowly here on such legal matters. I imagine it will eventually go to Andrea, but perhaps we will know by the time you come back."

Nick was surprised. "But that could be a long time."

Leah broke in: "I'll have to come back to testify, won't I?"

"Yes. At least *you* will. Perhaps not Nick. I have your statement and I'll be in touch with you about it. For now I think you need to rest and heal and plan for a wedding, no?" Nick and Leah smiled. The lieutenant nodded.

"You can both be happy. People here appreciate your work, Signor, they are excited that you care for the old traditions. And you"—he turned his gaze on Leah, who was pleased at the chance to look directly into his dark eyes—"the people here think you are very brave."

Leah smiled and blushed. "I'll play that for all it's worth."

Chapter Thirty-three

The day of the wedding dawned cold, but turned sunny by noon. In the high–ceilinged foyer of the theater, just off the piazza, long tables were covered with crisp white linen and laden with the local wines—dry red, light white, and sweet as well, breads, braided mozzarella cheeses with tomatoes, *Saturnella*, gorgonzola, octopus and grilled sardines, salamis, wide bowls of green salads, heaping trays of bananas, tangerines, and kiwi, trenchers of roasted lamb and chicken, olives, marinated chickpeas, and tray after tray of cakes, biscotti and chocolate custard tarts. The wedding cake, a custard fruit torte three feet across, sat in the middle of it all.

Dressed in smaller versions of their parents' dark three-piece suits and colorful knit dresses, boys and girls ran back and forth, chasing each other, screaming, and swooping by the tables like gulls after bread to grab a biscotti on the run. The adults milled around the room, laughing, chatting, moving to the table to refill their plates, and turning back to greet friends they hadn't seen since the autumn. The whole town had come.

Lieutenant Cavour approached Leah and extended his hand. "A fine thing, no? And you can feel the sense of relief that it is all over."

Leah smiled at him warmly. "Yes, and I thought you said bureaucracies moved slowly here."

Cavour nodded slowly, and patted her shoulder. Since the shooting, she and the lieutenant seemed to have developed a mutual, easy respect for one another. Leah went on. "And we have you, and many others: The mayor, the provincial office—which I think was also really your doing, Lieutenant—and Signor Scarpa here at the city office—which I think was also your doing—and Don Pietro—which as well may have been partially your doing—to thank. You said before that bureaucracies move slowly, but I think when you're in charge . . ."

"You're very kind, but—"

"No, don't deny it. I know how things work. And we appreciate it. Plus Maria at the flower shop, Sabina at the bar, Andrea and Silvio for the music, Giovanna for the wedding favors, the Signorine Marini at the restaurant, and, more than I can say, the Antoninis."

"Yes. The Antoninis do more for this town than you can imagine. You are fortunate to be their friends—they are some of the finest people alive, honest and true—as good as bread."

Leah nodded and fell silent for a minute thinking of them.

"But what I can't figure out is how Sara and Jonathan did it?"

Cavour grinned. "It was easy—well, sort of." Sara, followed close behind by Jonathan, appeared on Leah's other side and reached to shake hands with Cavour. "Hi, Lieutenant."

"Hello!" His attention was fully on Sara. "You look radiant"—then, embarrassed, he turned to Jonathan— "and I'll concede that Jonathan is looking very trim as well—though I think I am the more handsome." He winked at Sara and, taking her hand, bent to kiss it.

"Thank you. Jonathan *is* decked out!" She turned to her new husband. "You are certainly among the most hand-some, Lieutenant, but I think Jonathan may just have the edge." She put her hand to Jonathan's cheek.

Cavour's smile reflected a nostalgia of which Leah took note. "But, how *did* you arrange it all so quickly?"

Sara winked at Cavour and then smiled at her mother. "Don't be coy, Lieutenant. Most of the reason was be-cause you helped us. But there's another reason as well. We weren't in Prague when we called. We were in Flo-rence at the U.S. Consulate. We had already been to the Italian Consulate in San Francisco before we came, which was, I have to tell you, manned by a very unco-operative clerk."

Cavour nodded knowingly and laughed. "Never in?"

"Not only never in, he never returned our calls, and when he did have information that we needed, he never let us know. Anyway, from there on it was easy. The U.S. Consulate was nonchalant about the whole thing and signed the papers almost without looking . . . and from there, you know the rest."

"I'm sorry about the initial mix-up with the Don Eduardo. He has been with us so long, I had forgotten that he was not born in Italy and so could not marry you. It was a detail of law that slipped my mind."

"In the end, it didn't matter. Don Pietro was perfect— even if Jonathan and I didn't understand everything he knew enough English for the essentials. And the way Don Eduardo fixed the bells! Like a dream. They must have rung for a full thirty minutes!"

Leah interrupted. "But Sara, things went well here, but what about all the U.S. guests, all those invitations . . . what will happen?"

"I hadn't sent them. I only told you I had." She hugged her mother gently. "Well, I only sent a few, and those were for the reception we're having when we get back. With both of you here, how could I pass up a wedding in Italy?"

Chapter Thirty-four

A week after the wedding, Giovanna entered the dingy hallway, followed by the guard, who dangled keys in his hand. They passed three empty cells before they came to Angelina's. She was alone in the cell, lying on the cot on her back, her hands folded across her chest, staring at the ceiling. Giovanna cleared her throat, and the guard reached in front of her, opening the door.

Angelina tilted her head to the side. "Hey! It's you." She sat up slowly.

"Who else?" Giovanna stepped into the cell, with a glance back at the guard, who was already on his way out.

Angelina was dressed in a short-sleeved, baggy gray dress, with cloth slippers of the same drab gray on her feet. Giovanna shivered in the cold, still air of the cell, but Angelina appeared not to notice.

"So?"

"Nothing." Giovanna shrugged.

"What are you doing here?"

"I came to see you, obviously."

"Why?"

"I don't know." She looked around the cell and then sat on the bed beside Angelina. "I'm glad Giulio's dead."

"Yeah? Well, I wish you'd killed him instead of me, and then I wouldn't be here."

They both laughed, but Giovanna felt a tremor of fear up her back.

"Listen, you need anything?"

"What do you think? I need some decent clothes. And food—God, what swill they have been giving me! And I need Italo."

"Look, I don't want to argue. I just mean can I bring you anything? Shampoo? Soaps?"

Angelina's shoulders slumped. "No, nothing . . . I didn't really mean to do it, you know. I had just invited him on the walk to try to convince him that if he inherited to let me be the one to handle the sale."

"But why up the vie cave?"

"He was headed up there and I just tagged along, to try to keep talking with him."

"How did you know he was going to sell?"

"I didn't for sure, but I'd heard the scuttlebutt about him having a girlfriend down in Lazio, a girlfriend whose father owns a bar down there and that maybe he would be getting married and going down there to run the bar. It seemed perfect for everyone."

"So?"

"So, he got nasty. He said stuff about me and Italo—and about my father—said he wouldn't deal with a sneaking sleazy tramp like me, and I lost it."

Giovanna stared at the opposite wall.

Angelina spoke again. "Imagine! I got angry that he maligned my dad! My dad is a no-good, and imagine I got angry about it—about the truth!" She emitted a wild laugh, and then began to cry. "My God! My God!"

"But Signora Seta?"

Angelina sniffled and wiped her arm across her nose. "Same thing. I just wanted her to give me a chance, but she was worse than Giulio. She berated me for Italo, said she hoped Italo would never open a restaurant, that he didn't know anything about the town, was just a hanger-on, pretending to be a cowboy with his fake clothing and his lies about his grandfather knowing Tiburzi. The old biddy." Angelina's face twisted in hatred. "But the one I wish I could have gotten was that ugly American busybody, Leah."

"She wasn't following you. From what I heard it was just a coincidence."

"Not just that. She was flirting with Italo. These damned foreign women come in here ready for some sort of fling with Italian men so they can go back and write their travel articles about romance in Italy. God, she's the worst of all. I'd still like to get my hands on her."

Angelina's voice had risen with each sentence. She beat the edge of the bed with her fists and her face reddened.

Frightened, Giovanna rose to leave. "Listen, I've got to go. Guard! Guard!"

Angelina jumped to follow her, taking her by the arm. "Don't go. Just stay and talk a while." Her hair was disheveled and her face now blotched with red spots.

Giovanna tried to pull away, but Angelina held tightly. "I've got to get back to work. I'm helping Silvio in the shop now."

Loosening her grasp enough so Giovanna could slip out of it, Angelina, whispered, "That's good, Giovanna, that's good," and she began again to cry.

The guard sauntered through the doorway and approached, his keys at hand. With the barred door opened, Giovanna turned to Angelina. "I'll come back. I'll bring you some nice things." But she knew she was lying and would never see Angelina again.

Epilogue

The wedding over, and Sara and Jonathan back in the U.S. after their month-long honeymoon in Paris, Leah and Nick were relaxing with a cup of tea before they started to pack the last box of books to be shipped home.

"Overall, it's been a wonderful time, hasn't it?" She brushed her fingers across his hand.

"Yes, on the whole, wonderful—if you ignore the part about you being almost murdered—twice—and two people being actually murdered." He rolled his eyes.

"Oh, come on. I wasn't murdered. And I got my article done, with a little groveling because I was late, and you got some good interviews and photos for the book, with time left to actually finish it now and get full professor."

"Yes, full professor and then some relief from that pressure I hope."

They drank their tea. It was a few moments before Leah spoke.

"Nick?"

"Mmmm, good tea. What?"

"I got a letter from the magazine."

"They're paying you an extra five thousand dollars, the piece was so good."

"I wish."

"What?"

"They want me to do a piece on the Festival of St. Joseph."

"This year?"

"No, next."

"So, we'll have to come back. That's not bad. I'll teach summer and then take leave." He hesistated. "That is, if you're getting paid well."

Leah grinned. "I am, almost twice as much as for this one, and they're paying my airfare."

"Sounds perfect. Just don't get involved in any more murders."

"How could I? Two happening at once in such a small place will be enough for the next fifty years!"

"Don't curse yourself."

"Silly."

She tossed her head, laughing.

Nick regarded her. *If anything happens, she will be right in the center of it.*